Spirits' Gold

Spirits' Gold

John H. Paterson

This book is dedicated to the memory of my mother, Sally Paterson

Contents

London 2016

The Confession

Better come soon," read the text.

"*I'll be there tomorrow,*" I answered.

A "thumbs up" emoticon came back as a reply.

The rhythm of the train had been rocking me to sleep but the vibration of my cellphone had snapped me back to reality.

It was almost seven o'clock Tuesday morning. I was riding the tube on my way to work and I still had a few more stations to pass before mine. I checked tomorrow's train schedules online while the underground continued to rattle down the tracks. When it reached my station, I hurried up the stairs into the bright sunlight and walked briskly through the clean morning air to the high school.

"Good morning Miles," I said as I tapped on the open door beside the sign that read "Principal's Office." "I have a favor to ask."

Despite the early hour, Miles appeared to have been working for quite some time. He had his sleeves rolled up and his desk was piled high with stacks of paper. No one knew what time he arrived in the morning because he was always first. A big white mug perched on the edge of the desk displayed the words, "If you can read this, COFFEE ME."

"Good morning Kwame. Certainly. Come in."

"I have a sick friend and would like to visit him tomorrow. I know it's short notice, but do you mind if I take the day off?"

"Not at all," answered Miles. "If you lay out the program today, I'll find someone to supervise your classes tomorrow. Too bad about your friend," he added.

"Thanks," I said as I hurried off to prepare for my first class.

It didn't come as a surprise. Roland had been diagnosed with cancer of the spleen five or six months ago. I had talked to him on the phone a couple of times since then and had been meaning to make the trip down to their cottage near Bridgewater. It was clear that there was no more time for procrastinating if I was going to see my old friend once more.

I would have enjoyed some company on the trip, but it was a weekday and my wife Sofiya had to work and of course Jason had school. I caught the early train from Paddington Station to Bristol. Sitting alone on the train as it passed through the small towns and rolling countryside, I had time to think about Roland and our time together.

I changed trains in Bristol and arrived in Bridgewater just after eight o'clock. The bus brought me to the Cannington Post Office and I walked about fifteen minutes to their quaint stone cottage. It had a slate roof and was completely encircled by a low stone wall with a wooden gate. I walked up the path and tapped gently on the door. Jenny opened it looking as beautiful as ever, but tired. The stress of the last few months must have been hard on her.

"I'm so glad you could make it Kwame," said Jenny giving me a hug. "It means so much to Roland to see old friends. You especially."

"Thanks for the message and getting me moving. I've been meaning to come but never making the time."

The ancient cottage was small but had lots of windows. I had picked up some fresh cut flowers in Bridgewater and Jenny put them in a vase on the plain wooden table in the kitchen. It was a warm May morning and she had all the windows open and sun and fresh air filled the place. Roland was in the bedroom, asleep.

"He sleeps a lot," said Jenny. "The pain meds."

She put her hand on Roland's shoulder and squeezed it gently. Roland, who was now in his late eighties, looked gaunt and frail. The cancer had indeed taken its toll. But he opened his eyes and when he saw me he smiled and reached for my hand.

We propped him up with some pillows and I sat in the wooden arm chair with embroidered cushions at his bedside. Jenny left us and went to make tea.

"Thanks for coming Kwame. You are looking wonderful," he said in a hoarse whisper.

"Nice to see you too Roland. How are you feeling?" I asked while trying not to look shocked at the sight of his declining body.

"It's frustrating being stuck in this bed. And the doctor says I shouldn't be drinking whiskey. Not a good mix with the morphine." He lowered his voice, "Jenny gets me some anyway," he said with a chuckle. "It's a little late to be climbing on the milk wagon don't you think?"

I'd been preparing for this moment for months now. "Roland," I said putting my hand on his arm., "I want to thank you and make sure you realize how grateful I am for all you've done for me."

"Whatever I did was all my pleasure," he rasped. "I've enjoyed knowing you and your perseverance and success has been an inspiration to me and everyone around you."

He asked about me, my job and family. He listened intently as I spoke, and I could tell he was genuinely interested in how things were going. But I could tell he had something on his mind. Jenny brought tea and left us alone again. I steadied his cup as he drank the tea.

"Kwame. I want to tell you something before I die," he said staring at the ceiling. He paused, and his eyes moved to look at me and make sure I was paying attention. Then he said, "I killed the son-of-a-bitch. I shot him in the chest, three times!"

At first, I didn't know what to think. It struck me that perhaps the pain medication had muddled his thoughts. Neither of us said anything for a moment and then he continued. I listened and as he went on to fill in the details surrounding the incident and soon realized what he was talking about. I was aware of some of the events and circumstances, some I suspected and some, like this shooting, were a complete surprise to me. It seemed imperative for him to pass on this information and he pushed himself hard to get it out. He would talk a while, then rest, then talk some more. I continued to help him with his tea cup. When he finished saying what he needed to say, he drifted off to sleep. He seemed at peace now.

The clouds had gathered and a cool wind came up. We closed the windows and Jenny turned on the gas heater in the kitchen. We ate soup and sandwiches at the wooden table while he rested. I told her what Roland had relayed to me.

"He's been carrying that secret with him for twenty-five years now. Thank you for giving him the opportunity to get it off his chest. He really had no choice but to do what he did, and it doesn't really matter now. What's done is done. He just wanted you to know what happened."

We reminisced about the old days as we ate and laughed at some of the awkward circumstances we experienced. After we finished, I told her I would like to spend longer with Roland and felt badly but needed to leave to catch the train back to London. She asked me not to wake him and assured me that it was alright. Roland would wake and eat something later and she would bid him farewell for me. I told her I would return in a couple of weeks.

I was relieved. I really didn't want to have to say goodbye to him. I didn't want to face the finality.

Roland passed away the following week and a simple but beautiful service was held on Saturday at Cannington's Church of St. Mary. I had hired a car and drove down for the day with

Sofiya and Jason. The church was a stunning structure dating back to the fourteenth century. The beds bordering the church and pathways were loaded with spring flowers in full bloom. The setting was fitting for Roland.

Jenny kept herself together extremely well under the circumstances. Their marriage wasn't always what one would describe as harmonious, but they had been together for close to forty years. She would find the adjustment to being on her own extremely tough.

The turnout of friends and acquaintances was remarkable, and it was easy to see that Jenny appreciated them paying their respects and showing their support. After the service, the group gathered in the church hall for tea and snacks. The hall was cold, and the sound of the steel legged tables and chairs echoed off the painted brick walls and tiled floors. But it didn't stop everyone from sharing enthusiastically, stories about their experiences with Roland. Some were humorous anecdotes about his eccentricities and propensity for drinking and some were about his warm generosity to his fellow man.

As the group enjoyed each other's tales, I thought about mine. About my time with Roland. My story. And how it had never been properly shared.

When there was a lull in the proceedings, I stood up and said, "When I first met Roland I was fifteen years old and extremely fond of music. Living in a small village in West Africa, my opportunities were limited but Roland encouraged me and taught me to play piano. At the same time, he filled my head with tales of his travels and adventures. Today, due largely to his influence, I have an excellent job teaching music in a high school in London and have been able to see a lot of the world. Roland gave me the curiosity and desire to want to go out into the world and the self-confidence and encouragement to do it. He was a tremendous help to me and like everyone else here, I'll miss him big time."

But in a way, I felt like I'd cheated these people. Because that didn't begin to tell the story. The real story. What had happened all those years ago and miles away. About our time at the Chateau and the events that led up to and followed the killing of "the son-of-a-bitch." And how I ended up in England.

After the guests had left and we were helping tidy up, I cornered Jenny. "What would you think," I asked her, "about me putting the story together, of our adventures in the Ivory Coast, our time at Chateau Abengourou? Putting it on paper to share with others?"

She thought for a moment and I could see her mind reliving the events from so long ago. Her eyes looked distant and I was expecting her to discourage me from digging up the past. Then a smile came across her face and she turned to me and said, "That really was quite an adventure wasn't it? I think the idea is smashing. You should do it. And don't leave out a thing."

So, I started putting the story pieces together and tracking down anyone I could find that had been at Chateau Abengourou with us in 1991. I told them what I was doing, and they offered their help enthusiastically. I asked them to send emails detailing the events as they remembered them, and the response was overwhelming. Everyone had a slightly different version of what happened but they all remembered Roland and Jenny, and all wanted to help. Then I sifted through the emails and phone conversation records combining the details of their input with what I could remember myself and filling in the blanks as best I could. Slowly the pieces of the story of the Spirits' Gold came together.

Ivory Coast 1991

News of a Visitor

The fax machine came alive with a squealing squawking sound reminiscent of tuning a short-wave radio. When the connection was finally made, the printing started. Seated behind his desk, Roland looked up from the week-old London Times newspaper and wiped the perspiration from his forehead with a handkerchief as the ceiling fan pushed the sweltering air around the office. The paper grew in length in short spurts until suddenly the grunting sound paused as the paper cutter sliced off the first page allowing it to tumble into the tray. When the second page finished, a long sharp tone sounded, and the machine fell silent once again.

Roland pushed back his chair and maneuvered his stout frame across the room to retrieve the curled-up pages. He put on his glasses, spread the pages on his desk and studied them for a few seconds.

"Just what we need. Someone snooping around looking for problems. Just fucking lovely."

He was silent for a moment while he finished reading. "Brilliant. Just fucking brilliant. I knew something like this was going to happen."

"Kwame come in here." He removed his glasses and rubbed his eyes.

I had been cleaning the main floor hallway but dropped my mop immediately to hurry into the General Manager's office. Roland, in his mid-sixties, often looked like he'd slept in his clothes. And today was no different. His cheeks and nose were red, and his hair needed cutting and was sticking out in all directions. Sometimes he would put his feet up on his desk and when he got up, his shirt tails would be hanging out. But beneath the untidy exterior he was a warm kind man with warm kind eyes and everyone, or almost everyone, loved him.

"Kwame, please go and find Mr. Konaté and ask him to come and see me."

"Yes, Mr. Roland."

I hurried downstairs to the Operation Manager's office. He was an ill-tempered man who I avoided whenever possible. As it happened, he had someone in his office and I was afraid to interrupt him. So, I stood waiting in the doorway a moment.

He finally looked up at me and said "Are you just going to stand there like an idiot or are you going to tell me what you want? I'm not a mind reader."

"Mr. Konaté," I said nervously. "Mr. Roland would like to see you in his office."

Adjobi Konaté was physically intimidating. He was muscular to the point of being almost as wide as he was tall. His neck tapered from his shoulders to his ears truncating at the top of his shiny shaved head. He wore his shirt with several buttons undone and flashy gold chains draped down his chest. He sported enormous matching gold rings, one on each hand. Sweat rolled down his forehead and his white dress shirt clung to his soaking wet body becoming almost transparent.

Konaté was Ivorian but had spent several years working in the Ashanti Goldfields of neighboring Ghana. It was there that he gained his mining experience, and along with it, a heaping helping of conceit. The Ivory Coast had comparatively little mining history and this allowed him to brag about his knowledge and experience. He used this, as well as his physical stature to make himself stand out and intimidate others. Roland had hired him to oversee the day-to-day operations of the mine, which he did with an iron fist. He had an office in the Chateau and another at the mine but didn't live in the Chateau with the expatriates. He lived in a private house with his family in the city of Abengourou.

He was obviously annoyed at being interrupted and barked, "Can't you see I'm in a meeting you stupid boy? Tell him I will be along when I am finished."

"Yes sir. I'm sorry for the interruption sir."

I could see the visitor was the Head of Security, Lokossou Bamba. As I was leaving I heard Konaté say to Bamba, "I wish that drunken old fool would quit bothering me so I could get my work done."

I felt extremely uncomfortable being stuck between those two. Roland was a nice man. He had always treated me, and everyone else, well. It was true that he drank too much. But he didn't bother anyone. On the contrary, the more he drank the more stories he would tell. And I loved to listen to his tales. But Konaté had nothing but great disrespect for him. I had often heard Konaté lie to Roland and talk badly about him behind his back. But there was nothing I could do about it short of telling Roland what Konaté had said. And I wasn't about to do that. I wouldn't do anything to hurt Roland. I wished the Spirits would get rid of Konaté.

"Mr. Konaté said he will be here shortly," I said from the doorway of Roland's office.

I noticed he had poured some whiskey in his glass. It was three o'clock and he usually started around four or five. Probably the news in the fax had upset him. I went for ice.

On my way back from the kitchen I ran into Roland's wife, Jenny. She spotted the bucket of ice and said, "So the old boy is starting early today is he?"

She knew I didn't have an answer, so she continued, "Perhaps you would like to come to my room and spend some time with me Kwame? The old boy will have his nose stuck too deep in his whiskey glass to notice us. Your friend Afuom visits me sometimes. Perhaps he has told you about it?" she teased.

Jenny was quite pretty, short dark hair, tall and slim. Fifteen years younger than her husband, she had a reputation for flirting with the young men working in the Chateau. Afuom, the gardener's helper, had indeed told me about his encounters with her, and he seemed to be quite enjoying the experience. I didn't know how much was true and how much was Afuom's imagination but didn't want to have anything to do with Jenny. Her behavior made me feel uncomfortable and badly for Roland.

"I'm sorry Mrs. Jenny, I must finish my work or Nsia will be unhappy with me." I said putting the blame on the head housekeeper and rushed off down the hall.

I heard her giggle behind me and say, "Come and see me if you change your mind."

Jenny was Roland's second wife. He told me they met while working in Johannesburg for a large South African gold mining company. Jenny had been Roland's secretary when he was Vice President of Operations. The couple didn't have any children.

When I arrived at Roland's office, Konaté was there, reading the fax. When he finished he placed it back down on Roland's cluttered desk and said, "So what?"

I added ice to what remained of Roland's drink and put the bucket beside the bottle.

"So what? Are you crazy? This guy, Conner Jackson, is being sent here from Canada by the company's financial backers to look for flaws in our operation. What if he uncovers something here that we don't want uncovered? That's what." Roland picked up his glass and took a long pull.

I stepped back out to the hall to continue my cleaning but Roland's door was still open. I could see Konaté leaning back in his chair with his wrists resting on his belly and his fingers together in the shape of a roof.

"Relax Roland. He can't possibly find anything. I think you're giving this guy too much credit. He'll probably spend most of his time here drinking beer and chasing women. And besides, we've been extremely careful."

"Of course, we've been careful, but his job is to find things that we don't want anyone to find. That's what he does. And we must give him free rein," Roland said as he drained his glass.

"That's why I'm here. I know how to handle guys like this "Conner Jackson" fellow. I'll keep him on a short leash. You'll see."

"I'm sorry I don't share your confidence," Roland responded. "We don't want to end up with our balls in a ringer. I wish I never got mixed up in this."

Konaté leaned forward in his chair, stared at Roland for a moment and calmly said, "I'm afraid it's a little late for that Roland." Then he stood up and walked out of the office.

In the Beginning

Ihad only been working at the Chateau for a couple of months but had grown fond of it and most of the people living and working there. I was privileged to get this opportunity and didn't want anything the go wrong. If everyone was as easy to get along with as Roland, there wouldn't be a problem. But with characters like Konaté or Jenny, all manner of complications could arise. And I was terribly naïve in the ways of the world.

I grew up and still lived in a village of about two hundred people. We belonged to the Anyi tribe, part of the Akan, the largest of sixty tribes in the Ivory Coast. My father, Piesie, was the Chief or local Headman of our community. There was also a Council of Elders which acted as advisors who, along with my father would sit on their stools and talk and smoke and make decisions while the rest of the men labored in the palm oil or cacao plantations. The women and children carried water, collected firewood for cooking, washed the clothes and minded the younger ones.

"Kwame, play the dondo (talking drum) for your sisters and brothers," my mother would say while she was cooking and wanted the small ones entertained.

I would play traditional tribal songs and they would sing along. The older ones would be tending to the cassava garden or chickens and goats and the younger ones would sit in a semicircle on the ground in front of me. I could see my mother's lips moving as she sang along in the kitchen.

After each song the children would shout, "More Kwame, more." I would keep playing and singing until my mother finished cooking and my father arrived home. This was 1991 so there were no smart phones. We had an old black and white TV which picked up a couple of channels but music and playing soccer were our forms of entertainment. I loved to play the dondo as much as my brothers and sisters loved to listen.

Before we ate, my father would thank the Spirits for the food and our health and pour a little of his fermented rice wine on to the ground to share with our sacred ancestors.

There were seven children in our family. The number would have been nine but two never saw their first birthday. We referred to them as the two "gone but not forgotten." Malaria and meningitis were the two worst, but a multitude of other tropical diseases were there to challenge us. Akan children are not named until seven days after their birth to ensure that he or she has come to stay on earth and will not prematurely return to the "abode of the ancestors". Until that day, the child is regarded as a stranger. My little brother died of malaria at four months and my little sister succumbed to tetanus after living only five days. As much as we grieved for our lost siblings, we accepted their fate as the wishes of the Spirits. And we were comforted to know that they were now living with the Spirits and watching over us. That being said, I knew my mother still had an ache in her heart when she remembered the two babies she lost. On their birthdays she be quiet and melancholy. Sometimes I would find her crying and would do my best to cheer her up, and I'd encourage my brothers and sisters to do the same.

Although I was the oldest, I was not in line for the position of the next Chief. It was tradition that the first son of the Chief's oldest sister would be successor. This was the only way to be one hundred percent sure that the blood line was continued.

What we lacked in possessions, we made up for with tradition and rituals.

I, like my brothers and sisters, had attended the local elementary school. But because I did so well, I was permitted to continue to high school, or a shortened version of it, that I had just completed. I loved to learn and would read books whenever I got an opportunity.

When the mining company announced the development of a gold mine close to our village, it was all anyone could talk about. Was it a good thing or bad? There would surely be more jobs. Better pay? Would we be rich? Would it hurt the environment? Would cutting the trees of the forest upset the Spirits of our ancestors? It was their home after all. My father and the Elders had their work cut out for them deciding how to proceed. There was going to be a lot of talking and smoking.

Negotiations between the company and the village finally resulted in the mine getting the "green light," but several conditions were attached. First, the company was required to pay the village an ongoing lease fee which was expected to keep the Spirits satisfied. The mine would also provide work for any or all the men of our village that wanted it. To compensate for the loss of wildlife habitat, the company purchased and donated a parcel of land, equal in size to ten times the area that they would be disturbing to be used as a wildlife sanctuary. But first, a sacrifice was needed.

The Sacrifice

The project was going to be large and disruptive and we knew the Spirits would not be pleased. Cutting the trees in the forest would upset them enough but at least they would grow back. What we didn't know was how they would react to having their gold stolen. Mined, processed and shipped out of the country for good. So, a sacrifice on a large scale would be required to appease them. And, of course, the mining company would pay for it all. My father and the Elders worked on the list of things they felt would make the Spirits happy. When they agreed that enough was included to placate those whose resting place would be disturbed, the list was presented to the company. The company's protests couldn't deny the logic that if the Spirits were not happy, there was no way they would let the project go ahead. Nothing good can come from cutting corners on a sacrifice. Especially when someone else is paying for it.

Preparations were made. The list included the equivalent of a few hundred eggs, two dozen chickens, six goats, and a cow as well as six cases of Malawi gin. We supplied the livestock and the company paid us a good price. They bought our eggs, chickens and goats as well as those of our neighbors. And it could be expected that our benevolent Spirits would be happy to share what was left over with us.

Most people in our village proclaimed to be Christians but they also followed their traditional religion which worshipped the Spirits of our ancestors and the animals of the forest. Our local priest wasn't that thrilled about the event but there was nothing he could do. They say that his predecessor died at the hands of the Spirits, so he wouldn't want to get on their bad side. Apparently, he died of blood poisoning because of cuts inflicted while cleaning his teeth with a razor blade. It seems the Spirits bumped his elbow in retaliation for something he did or said.

Almost everyone from our village as well as visitors from the nearby communities came to the site of the proposed mine to watch and participate in the sacrifice. We waited in the shade of the huge trees surrounding a clearing in the forest that was to host the activities. My father and the Elders wore their traditional dress. The robes, spears and masks were colorful, and the drumming and chanting set the mood of anticipation and excitement.

Anyone who has ever been to an Anyi sacrifice will tell you how deeply involved the spectators become. The shouting and waving and cheering grows in intensity as the different levels of offerings are reached. The atmosphere is exhilarating.

The eggs were passed around, so everyone could take part in paying tribute to the Spirits. The goats and cow were tethered close to a circle of rocks on the ground. This was the area where the sacrifices were to be made. The word was given, and everyone took turns throwing their eggs on the ground in the circle and chanting offerings to the Spirits, often directed toward deceased family members. The crowd would shout and cheer in support of the offerings.

Once the eggs had all been broken, the crowd's attention turned to the chickens. This was the highlight of the day because it involved the most action. The chickens were taken from a pen to the sacrifice ring, one-by-one, to have their heads chopped off by a machete wielding Elder. This caused the crowd to go wild because the headless chickens were released to run through the crowd. Those fortunate enough to be spattered by blood from a headless chicken were blessed. The process was repeated twenty-four times and it turned into quite a frenzy. As the chickens finally died, they were collected and returned to the ring.

I won't go into the details of the passing of the goats and finally the cow. The carcasses, along with the gin, were left in the waning daylight for the Spirits as the spectators returned to their homes. But when the sun rose the next morning, there were no remains to be found. Suffice it to say that whatever the Spirits didn't carry off into the forest, the locals took care of. The people of the village ate well for the next several days. And my father and the elders got a nice change from their rice wine.

Devastating Development

No scenario we imagined came anywhere near to the magnitude and degree of devastation we witnessed. We watched in awe while the great machines bulldozed the trees and levelled the hills. The thunderous crashing and snapping of towering ancient tree trunks was overwhelming. Deafening. Our hearts broke as we watched the birds flying away and other animals fleeing the destruction. I felt that day that I had lost something I would never get back. I felt like we had been tricked. Had my father and the Elders made the wrong decision? I think they realized that progress was inevitable so the best they could do was to position the village to benefit as much as possible from the development. But I don't think they had any idea as to the extent of the damage. We were simple people and terribly innocent in the ways of the world.

The weeks passed, and the construction crews battled Mother Nature. The rains turned the iron rich soil into sloppy red mud which attempted to swallow the heavy machinery. Torrential downpours washed the mud into the rivers, raging blood red. A few trees were salvaged for lumber, but most were bulldozed into piles and burned using old tires and diesel fuel to drive the flames.

Eventually, when most of the clearing and levelling was out of the way, the mine started to take shape. The office building, process plant and repair shop rose to replace the forest. Vast plastic lined leach pads stretched as far as the eye could see and ponds as big as soccer fields were excavated to house the cyanide solution used to extract the gold. This would be a true test of the patience and cooperation of the Spirits.

Finally, an eight-foot-high chain link fence was built around the entire operation. The sign beside the front gate read "Golden Sunshine Mining Company – Abengourou Mine Site-Authorized Personnel Only"

The upside was that there was now a protected wildlife sanctuary to house animals being displace by activities such as the development of the mine or the destruction of the rainforest by the cacao and palm oil farmers. Deforestation was causing many species to become endangered through loss of habitat. It was named Sanctuaire de Faune de l'or, Wildlife Sanctuary of Gold.

The sanctuary surrounded the mine and was completely fenced to keep the wildlife in and hunters out. The Ministry of the Environment acted as administrator and often brought animals that had been confiscated from poachers or people who possessed them illegally and released them into the Sanctuary. There was also a facility where animals that had been injured could be treated by a veterinarian and released after they had recovered.

I was fifteen years old at the time and too young to work in the mine, so I volunteered at the Sanctuary. Mostly cleaning cages and helping the vet feed the animals. One day, a Wildlife Protection Officer arrived in a pick-up truck with a cage in the back. Inside was a young leopard. He had been hit by a car and appeared to have been shot. He was almost unconscious from loss of blood.

It was speculated that the animal was being pursued by poachers who wanted his skin and ran out onto the road to escape but was struck by a car. A crowd gathered at the scene of the accident and someone had the sense to contact the Ministry.

The bone in his leg was fractured and would require a cast and a long time to heal. The officer and I watched as the vet examined the injured animal.

"The Animal Rehabilitation Facility is not equipped to accommodate a leopard," said the vet. "It would be cruel to keep a cat his size in a small cage like that. Unfortunately, the best thing to do, the most humane, will be to put the animal down."

I was devastated at the thought of this magnificent animal being destroyed.

"We could build a special enclosure," I pleaded. "The people of the village could help."

"Perhaps, but how would we feed him?" asked the vet. "It will be a long time before he will be able to hunt for himself and leopards have huge appetites."

"My friends and I could set traps and catch bush rats for him."

He could see how eager I was to save the injured cat and agreed to give it a try. He sewed up the bullet wound and set the broken bone. The next morning my father assembled a team of men from the village and built an enclosure. They cut bamboo poles from the jungle and managed to convince the mining company to donate some left-over fencing. My friends and I built a lean-to inside the enclosure to shelter and protect him from the sun and rain. We set wire snares to catch bush rats and other creatures roaming the forest floor. By the end of the day, the animal's new home was ready with a tasty dinner waiting inside for him. He hopped in on three legs, devoured the rodents and went to sleep in the lean-to.

We named him "Okwan" which meant "found on the road." He learned my voice and when he heard me call his name he would come to me. We became good friends, but always with a strong fence between us.

It was customary for young men to start working in the plantations at age sixteen, but the work was hard, and the conditions were poor. The workers were exposed to pesticides, machete accidents and even poisonous snake bites. The mine had a rule that required employees to be at least eighteen years of age. I was expecting to spend a couple of years tending cacao trees before working at the mine when one day my father asked Roland if he could make an exception in my case. Roland told my father that working at the mine was out of the question but kindly offered to let me try working as a house boy at the Chateau.

When my father came home for dinner that night, he broke the news.

"Kwame has a job working at the mining company's Chateau. He will need some decent clothes," he announced. "We want him looking his best."

And so, it was that I went to work at Chateau Abengourou which was about a half hour bus ride from our village. My mother bought me a new set of clothes and gave me strict instructions to keep them clean. And bright and early Monday morning, I was off on a new adventure. One that would change the course of my life.

The Chateau

The Chateau was set well back on the property with a stone driveway culminating in a circle in front of a pillared entrance. The grounds, manicured with beautiful lawns and flowering shrubs and trees, were a stunning contrast to the neighboring properties which were much more modest. Behind the vanilla colored building, the ground sloped downward and the Chateau became three stories opening on to a large swimming pool bordered by hedges.

The Chateau was built by the late Minister of Tourism who used it as his country house and a place to entertain guests. He was the one to name it Chateau Abengourou, after the city in which it was located. Abengourou had a population of about one hundred thousand, the largest interior city in the country. The name "Abengourou" stems from the Akan language expression "n'pé kro", which means "I don't like long discussions." The name was also chiseled into the concrete above the building's main entrance. When he died, the Minister's widow couldn't afford to maintain it or didn't want to, so she put it up for sale. The mining company bought the Chateau and used it to house expatriate management and visiting dignitaries. Its architecture was reminiscent of the proud colonial estate mansions of the American South except that it was constructed of concrete instead of wood. And the windows, though large, were made of dozens of smaller panes separated by wooden divisions.

It had five suites on the second floor, each complete with sitting room and bathroom. The General Manager's residence and office were on the main floor as were the formal dining room, drawing room and library. The lower level housed the offices, games room, main dining room, kitchen and staff quarters.

I got off the bus and walked up the hill to the Chateau. My father had described it to me but it's size and beauty far surpassed the picture my imagination had painted. "What was I in for?" I had no idea what my job would entail and had no experience other than tending animals and gardening. I was nervous and starting to have doubts about working there. There was a crowd milling around the gate. Apparently, all trying to find work. I made my way up to the front.

"My name is Kwame Kouassi," I told the guard. "I am to start work today as a house boy."

The guard looked at his list, nodded and opened the man door in the wrought iron fence just enough for me to squeeze in without the throng following.

"Your entrance is around back, by the kitchen," he said and pointed to a pathway leading around to the side of the building.

The head housekeeper, Nsia, met me as I entered the kitchen. She looked me up and down like she was deciding whether or not to keep me and finally said, "Well you're tall so we'll have someone to reach the high shelves, and you're skinny, so you probably don't eat too much. I guess we can give you a try."

Nsia was only a little over five feet tall so it was easy to see why she would appreciate having someone tall around to reach high places. But she ran a tight ship and despite her small stature, she had everyone doing exactly as she instructed.

I learned the etiquette, the routines, and the likes and dislikes of the people staying in the Chateau and did my best to keep out of trouble.

Roland (the staff called him Mr. Roland) would laugh and joke with the Chateau staff was and was well liked. He would always make time for us if we had questions. Originally from England, he spent several years in the British Army but later lived in South Africa. For many years he was Vice President of a large mining company in Johannesburg. But the years caught up with him and certain company problems were blamed on him. He ended up being forced to retire. An expensive divorce settlement with his first wife and some bad investment decisions along the way had eroded his financial resources. It was because of this, that Roland needed an ongoing income to make ends meet. The job of general manager was a step down from his former position, but he was older and beyond the peak of his career. The mining company hired him mainly to be a liaison between the mine, the community and the government agencies. He was good at entertaining and winning people over but didn't pay much attention to detail.

There was a beautiful old piano in Roland's sitting room and he enjoyed playing it at parties. He was extremely talented. When he found out that I liked music he started teaching me how to play. Sometimes I would practice in the late afternoon and he would drink his whiskey and tell stories of his experiences in the army or South Africa or his early life in England. He described the places in such vivid detail that I would imagine I was there. I was fascinated, and it instilled in me a desire to travel. A desire which grew the more time we spent together.

"Do you think it's possible for a poor boy from a small village to visit other countries?" I asked.

"Of course, it's possible. All you need to do is work hard and grasp opportunities," answered Roland. "The Lord helps those who help themselves."

Around our little village, no one ever moved more than a few kilometers away. Usually only to marry a girl from the next village. When I told my father I would like to see the world, he told me not to talk such nonsense. He said our village was the home of our ancestors and our family home. And the Spirits wouldn't be happy if I left. And they wouldn't be happy if they heard me talking that way. I didn't bring it up with him again. I knew he loved me and wanted to see our family together. But it didn't change my mind.

The Visitor Arrives

Acouple of days after the fax with the news of his impending visit, Conner Jackson arrived. I was washing Roland's Jeep when a shiny new Land Cruiser drove up the driveway. I was on my way up to Roland's office before it came to a stop.

"Mr. Roland," I said catching my breath. "A big car just arrived. A driver with two men. One black, one white."

"Thanks Kwame," replied Roland as he got up to go downstairs and meet the guests. "Please come along, I'd like your help with the bags."

As Roland came outside, he recognized the well-dressed black man as Leon Djedje, the Minister of Energy and Mines. He hadn't met the other man who was tall and broad shouldered, with disheveled sandy reddish hair and a three-day beard. He looked to be about thirty-five years old and Roland correctly pegged him as Conner Jackson.

It was about four o'clock and the rain was just starting. The visitors congregated under the roof of the entrance to the Chateau for protection.

"Leon, welcome, what a surprise!" Roland greeted shaking his hand.

"Nice to see you Roland. I hope you don't mind. My old friend Conner needed a ride, so I thought I'd play taxi. Conner Jackson, Roland Wells."

The two shook hands and Roland graciously welcomed Conner to Chateau Abengourou.

"Leon, you must have dinner with us and spend the night. You can fill us in on how you two came to be friends. It will be too late to drive back to Abidjan and I will not take no for an answer." demanded Roland.

"If you insist. But please don't go to any trouble on my part."

"Nonsense, no trouble. We must have a proper welcome dinner for Mr. Jackson anyway. Come on then, Kwame please bring their suitcases to their rooms."

Conner extended his hand to me and with a warm smile said, "Nice to meet you Kwame, I'm Conner."

"My pleasure," I said.

From that moment, I had a feeling we would get along well.

Against my protests, Conner, who was at least six-foot-four, picked up his large knapsack and hoisted it over his shoulder. I ended up carrying only the Minister's small overnight bag.

Everyone living or staying at the Chateau had been invited to the dinner. They arrived one by one for drinks by the pool at around six-thirty. The sun had gone down, so the oppressive heat was easing up. Roland, as the host, welcomed everyone and introduced Conner. You could tell Roland enjoyed this part of his job best and did it very well.

Leon said a few words in Anyi and poured a bit of his drink on the patio as an offering to the Spirits. Some of the others did the same.

"Before I forget, Roland, the concession you applied for is getting extremely close to being approved," said Leon. The file has moved from the environmental department to the legal department. Next stop is my in-basket for the final signature."

"We appreciate your attention to the application Leon. The additional land means a lot to our future operations here."

Nsia had asked me to help with the dinner so I was serving hors d'oeuvres.

"This is my wife, Jenny," said Roland introducing her to Conner. "She works tirelessly to ensure the staff are keeping the Chateau running like a clock."

Jenny was all dressed up and ready for a party. Conner noticed she was smiling at him while checking him out from top to bottom.

"This place is truly remarkable Jenny," said Conner. "You should be commended."

"Thank you, Conner," replied Jenny with a glint in her eye. "Just let me know if you need anything."

Roland said, "There is someone else here I'd like you to meet. I'll be right back" When he stepped away, Jenny stepped closer. So close in fact that her body rubbed up against Conner's, and she whispered in his ear, "Anything at all."

"Thanks Jenny," Conner said stepping back just enough to break contact. "I think I'll be fine."

"I think you'll be great," she smiled.

"That's all I need," thought Conner. "To get fired from the job for carrying on with the General Manager's wife."

"Conner, I'd like you to meet Lyla Townsend. Lyla is the Process Plant Manager," said Roland looking quite proud of himself.

Conner did his best to conceal his enthusiasm at meeting the prettiest Plant Manager he'd ever come across. Her accent was unmistakably Australian. The introduction put an abrupt end to Jenny's advances, which was likely what Roland had planned. This was not the first time he had had to intervene in his wife's dalliances. It was obvious that Jenny's enthusiasm about Lyla's arrival was markedly less than Conner's.

The other dinner guest, Michael Vandoorn arrived.

Michael noticed my platter of breaded shrimp and stuffed mushrooms as he walked in and helped himself to a handful on his way over to the group.

"Michael is the Mining Manager," Roland said by way of introduction.

Michael was about six-foot-five and as skinny as a rail. When he smiled he showed off an enormous set of bright white teeth that reached from ear to ear. Friendly and jovial and when he finished swallowing his mouthful, he greeted Conner with a strong South African accent.

Michael wiped his hand on his pants and shook Conner's with great enthusiasm. He looked to be in his early forties. Roland mentioned that Michael had been at the project for about a year and had a wife in Cape Town whom he visited on his time off.

Leon joined the conversation and told everyone that he and Conner had been good friends since they were in graduate school together in Canada. When he arrived in Canada, he didn't know a soul. He met Conner the first day as they were assigned to share a graduate student office. Conner introduced Leon to all his friends and made him feel entirely welcome. Ten years later he still kept in touch with many of them and some had visited him in the Ivory Coast.

"Oh yes," agreed Conner. "Everyone loved Leon. Especially once they got used to him sharing his drinks with the Spirits. The other students had trouble with beer being poured on the ground."

The Chateau residents normally ate in the downstairs dining room but that night they enjoyed a delicious fish dinner, accompanied by fine French wines, in the General Manager's dining room which was reserved for special occasions such as this.

On nights that I worked late, I slept on a bunk in the staff quarters because the buses had stopped running and I would be starting work early in the morning.

After dinner, Conner and Leon drank brandy in the games room and talked about old times. Roland had gone to bed but asked me to stick around and make sure they had everything they wanted.

"I'm surprised you haven't gotten married," said Leon. "Haven't met the right girl or was your experience in the Yukon enough to put you off for good?"

"Haven't been looking actually. Not because of what happened before, but I've been having too much fun travelling the world with my work. No commitments. Just do what I want. Besides, there are lots of fish in the sea."

"Like the Plant Manager? I saw you checking her out."

"I must say that meeting her was a pleasant surprise. How about you? You happy? Don't you miss being single?"

"Wouldn't have it any other way," Leon replied. "Wonderful wife and two great kids. Even though the three of them drive me crazy sometimes."

Leon took a sip of his brandy and said, "Conner, I should tell you something. There are rumors that there may be a coup attempt in our country in the near future. The President, who is a good friend of mine, comes from a wealthy cacao farming family. He has done much for the country regarding stabilizing the business environment and encouraging foreign investment. This has increased the tax base and provided funds for desperately needed social programs. He is extremely popular with most of the voters."

"But he's worried. Not just for his own personal safety but for the wellbeing of the people of the Ivory Coast. The Chief of staff of the army, Major General Tiémoko is a greedy and powerful man. It appears that he wants control of more than just the army. He has his own ideas about how the country should be run and wants access to the Treasury. Some people believe he is planning to overthrow the government. He reports to the Minister of Defense but has the backing of the army more than the Minister does. His staff are extremely loyal to him, or fearful of him but either way, will do pretty well anything he orders. The reason I bring it up with you is because Tiémoko has quite strong ties to the mine."

"What kind of ties?" asked Conner.

"Tiémoko provides contract security services to the mine using army personnel. It's a way Tiémoko supplements his income and possibly finances his other objectives. The mine's Head of Security reports directly to Tiémoko. Tiémoko visits here quite often. The Operations Manager, Adjobi Konaté is married to the General's sister, which is how he got his foot in the door in the first place. I need your help with this. I'd like you to keep your ears and eyes open for any suspicious goings on."

"Like what?"

"At this point I really don't know. I would like to know anything you can come up with. What type of relationship exists between Golden Sunshine Mining and Tiémoko? Is it strictly the security contract or is there something else? Any routine schedules or sudden changes to schedules. Anything out of the ordinary. And, I just thought you should be aware who you are dealing with."

"This is shaping up to be more interesting than my normal due diligence assignments," said Conner finishing his brandy. "I'll see what I can find out and let you know."

"And let me know if you need anything from me," said Leon. "But most important, watch your back my friend."

Gossip

The sun rose at about five-thirty. Conner was already awake and used the time he had before breakfast was served to go for a walk around the grounds and enjoy the fresh air. I was out feeding kitchen scraps to the goat and a baby bottle of milk to the monkey. The gardener had tethered the goat in the orange grove. The monkey was sitting on her back.

"What do we have here?" asked Conner as he picked an orange and cut it into quarters with his pocket knife.

"The monkey's mother was killed by a hunter. We took her in and she's become emotionally attached to the goat. It's like they are family. She rides on her back most of the day. She drinks milk from a bottle now, but we plan to teach her to use a cup when she's older."

Conner shared his orange with me and helped feed the goat. Then he took some photos of the pair with his camera. As he continued his walk around the property, Conner saw Lyla come out of the front door of the Chateau and wave as she set off down the driveway and along the road for her morning run.

Leon had left early to get back to Abidjan and Lyla seldom ate breakfast, so the only other person eating that morning was Michael Vandoorn. They talked a bit about the mining operation and arranged to meet at the mine later. They were almost finished when Michael changed the subject.

"What did you think about Roland's wife?" asked Michael grinning and lowering his voice.

Conner picked up what he meant and answered, "She seems quite friendly."

"Yes, she loves to tease but she's actually pretty harmless. They say she's settled down a lot over the years. I know some of the people that she and Roland worked with in Johannesburg where apparently, she earned quite a reputation."

Michael went on to explain that Jenny and Roland started seeing each other while he was still with his first wife. "And by seeing each other, I mean spending a lot of time in Roland's office with the door closed."

Conner sipped his coffee and listened while Michael shoveled in his last bite of eggs and went on. He seemed to be enjoying the opportunity to spread some gossip to new ears.

"Anyway, I guess the first wife got wind of the affair and figured that everyone was laughing at her behind her back. So, one day she shows up at the mining company offices and demands to see him. The receptionist tries to stop her and says he's in a meeting but the wife's determined. She finds his door closed but not locked. You see, the individual offices don't have locks to discourage this type of thing from happening. But these two lovers weren't to be deterred and Roland had pushed a big chair up in front of the door. Well, the wife puts her shoulder into it, the chair tips over, the door flies open and there are Roland and Jenny, on Roland's desk, naked as Jay birds. Going at it like a couple of wildebeests."

Michael was laughing hard by now but had to get the rest of the story out. His voice was getting higher and higher and a few bits of scrambled eggs were flying out of his mouth as he neared the end.

"To add insult to injury, the receptionist and a few other employees came running over when the wife was struggling with the door, so when it flew open, there was quite an audience all of whom managed to catch a glimpse of the show," Michael finished by slapping his hand on his leg and laughing some more. "That was the talk of the office for some time. I guess she took him to the cleaners in the divorce settlement."

"An expensive bit of "afternoon delight" wouldn't you say Conner?" Michael added as he was regaining his composure.

"I'll bet he won't do that again," replied Conner.

Bamba and the Gold Room

Konaté arrived at the Chateau and went to see what Roland had learned about Conner's plans.

"Not much at this point," said Roland. "Last night was mostly small talk and pleasantries. It sounds like he's planning to stay about a week. I'll continue playing the good cop and you can be the bad cop."

"Well don't make him too comfortable with your generous hospitality. We want him out of here and on his way back to Canada as quickly as possible," Konaté replied and left to go to his own office.

A few minutes later, Conner arrived at Roland's office. The door was open as usual.

Tapping on the door jamb and said, "Good morning Roland."

"And to you," replied Roland rising and pointing to a chair in front of his cluttered desk. "I trust you slept well?"

"Definitely," Conner said as he sat down. "After all the travelling, the wonderful dinner and all that wine, it would have been impossible not to."

"Then tell me how I can help you carry out your assignment here," said Roland.

"I'd like to start by meeting with all the department heads individually to get a feel for the whole operation," explained Conner. "Then I'll focus on the areas I consider to be most critical."

"Perfect, let's start by me introducing you to our Operations Manager, Adjobi Konaté."

Roland led Conner downstairs to Konaté's office and tapped on the open door. Konaté was working on something but looked up for a second, then gave a sigh, put down his pen and looked at his watch while he stood up.

"Good morning Roland, nice to see you," he said with a broad grin that looked forced. "And this must be the great Conner Jackson everyone is talking about."

He shook Conner's hand and squeezed it harder than necessary. "Nice to meet you Mr. Jackson or is it ok if I call you Conner."

"Well if you call me Mr. Jackson, you are going to be the only one who does, so, yes, please call me Conner."

"Ok then Conner, how can I help you?"

"Conner would like to start by meeting all the department heads," interrupted Roland. "He has already met Michael and Lyla, so that leaves the Accounting, Maintenance and Security department heads. Do you think you could arrange that for me?"

"Certainly. And Conner, we will provide you with all the information you require to do your job," said Konaté. "But I think you will soon see that everything here is in order and transparent. I run a tight ship, so your employer is wasting his money having you turning over rocks looking for flaws. How long do you plan to be here?"

"I have budgeted a week but can stay longer if necessary, if I find anything under those rocks," said Conner digging back at Konaté a little.

"Well if you get tired of turning over rocks and not finding anything, the company has a beach house you are welcome to use for a few days. Perhaps we could even find some young lady to "cook and clean" for you."

"I didn't come all this way to relax at the beach Adjobi. Are you trying to keep me away from the operation for some reason?" Conner asked.

"Ha," laughed Konaté. "You will see. I don't put up with anything less than perfect. I have no patience with people who don't measure up to my standards."

Roland left the two and returned to his own office. Conner went with Konaté who introduced him to the head of the Accounting department whose office was also in the Chateau. Conner requested copies of some reports and they left to drive to the mine. They chatted on the way and Konaté asked about Conner's background.

Conner explained that he had graduated from Mining Engineering when he was twenty-three and went to work in a zinc mine for a couple of years. He returned to school for another year to do a master's degree which is where he met Leon Djedje. After that he started doing contract work for mining consulting companies in Toronto, learning the business and making contacts. For the last five years he had been consulting exclusively on his own.

Conner asked about Konaté's background and he explained that he had earned a business degree at the University of Abidjan and had gone to work in Ghana where he could make more money. He ended up with a mining company that realized he had a flair for managing people and made him a mine foreman. He spent ten years working at various operations around the Ashanti Goldfields in positions of increasing responsibility.

"When I was Mine Superintendent at one operation, I would take each new hire in my pick-up and park on the hill overlooking the mine," Konaté explained. "I'd point out the mine gate and say, "Working here is simple. There are only two ways to do things, my way or straight out that gate,'" he laughed. "No one fucked around with me."

"When I heard about the Abengourou Mine opening, I applied for the job and Roland hired me. He wanted someone that would keep the operation running smoothly so he wouldn't have to concern himself with it. And you'll see. I do a good job. The place runs like a well-oiled machine."

As they drove through the main gate of the mine, Konaté pointed out the office building on the left, the Process Plant on the right and the Maintenance Shop straight ahead with a gravel covered yard in the center of the three buildings.

First, they went to the shop and met with the Manager of Maintenance. Like the accounting department, it wasn't a probable place to find crucial operational flaws. They chatted briefly and left.

Next, they went to the office building to meet with Lokossou Bamba, the head of security. Konaté introduced them and left to see to other business.

Bamba was tall and slim with prominent cheekbones and large protruding eyes. Speaking slowly and with a deep voice, he annunciated each word. Probably around fifty years of age, he'd been in the army for thirty years where he had worked his way up slowly. He was dressed in fatigues and carried a pistol in a holster on his belt.

Bamba explained that the mine had a security contract with a company controlled by General Tiémoko using army personnel. Conner didn't let on that he was already aware of the fact.

"Our recruits are better trained, more disciplined and more reliable than those of private security firms," he explained. "Plus, we have forces around the entire country to find and apprehend a thief if there were ever to be an incident," he said.

"Very impressive," said Conner. "And have you had any incidents?"

"None," said Bamba. "It would be suicide. Let me show you around."

Bamba led Conner to the Security Monitoring Room which was a fitting name because it had video monitors all over the wall. The cameras were trained on the Process Plant, the Gold Room, the leach pads and ponds, the front gate and the parking lot as well as many other locations around the mine site. A young man in uniform watched carefully and had several radios and alarm switches within reach.

"We have forty-eight cameras around the property." He explained. "Nothing happens here that we don't know about. Let me show you the Gold Room."

They crossed the yard to the Process Plant which was a beige, steel-clad building similar to the Maintenance Shop. It was mostly open inside with various pieces of equipment connected by stairs and catwalks. In the corner was a squat concrete structure. The Gold Room.

Bamba described the structure as they walked over to have a closer look.

"The walls are poured reinforced concrete and the door is made of half-inch thick steel plate." A large tumbler and bolt mechanism kept the door secure. "Only Lyla Townsend, the Plant Manager and I have access. We each have different combinations and all entrances are recorded on the security computer."

Bamba walked up to the door and worked the tumbler back and forth. There was a click and he slid the bolt back opening the door.

They walked in and saw the furnace where the concentrated gold was melted and poured into bricks. There was also the table, like a big steel workbench, where the bricks were cleaned, stamped and sampled. Beside the table was the slag bucket which contained shiny glassy rock fragments with small blobs of gold splattered throughout. On the floor were several plastic bags containing black sludge.

"The slag is what is left over from cleaning the gold bars from our last pour and will be added to the furnace at our next pour," Bamba said pointing to the bucket of glassy material. "We also store the electro winning precipitate that goes in the furnace to make the gold bars here," he added pointing to the bags. "It doesn't look like much, but each bag is actually contains over one hundred thousand dollars' worth of gold."

"When will the next pour be?" Conner asked.

"I'm not sure, we don't stick to a schedule for obvious security reasons," he replied. "And we don't make a practice of storing any gold here. The gold is picked up by armored car directly after it is poured. As soon as it has cooled enough to be handled, it is taken to Abidjan and flown by commercial jet to the refiner in Belgium. As it goes out the gate, it becomes the responsibility of the armored car company and is fully insured. But we still avoid getting in a routine which would make it easier for a robbery attempt."

"How many security staff do you have?" asked Conner.

"We have four men per shift and four shifts for a total of sixteen."

They walked outside on the way back to the office building and Bamba pointed out the Security Barracks. A long plain building just past the leach ponds.

"So that's about it unless you have any more questions," said Bamba.

"No, not now," answered Conner. "But I would like to say I'm impressed with your operation here. Does your firm provide security for any other mines?"

"Not at this time. Although there are numerous artisanal operations around the country, there is only one other mine operating currently and they have their own security personnel. However, I understand that Golden Sunshine Mining has plans to grow and I know Major General Tiémoko would like to provide security services for future operations."

Bamba showed Conner the way to Michael Vandoorn's office which was down the hall from his own.

"Perfect timing," said Michael. "I was just about to head out to the pit and check on the operation. Please join me."

They hopped in Michael's pickup and Michael gave Conner a tour of the open pit mine and crushing operations. The rock drills would bore holes into the granitic rock and the holes were loaded with explosives. The rock was then blasted and loaded into trucks with one hundred tonne payloads by enormous hydraulic shovels. The ore was hauled from the massive open pit to the stockpile at the crusher and the waste rock was hauled to sprawling dumps. The operation ran twenty-four hours a day.

"How have production levels been? Have you been hitting targets?" Conner inquired.

"Spot on. The equipment is new and has the capacity to do the job. We've been crushing seventeen thousand tonnes a day quite consistently. Some days more, and still have time to do our maintenance."

"I'll bet that keeps head office happy," replied Conner.

"Importantly yes," said Michael as he maneuvered his pickup under the conveyor exiting the crusher. As a matter of fact, that was Roland's downfall at his last job. As Vice President of Operations, he had the managers of three mines reporting to him. It was Roland's responsibility to ensure that corporate targets were met. One mine was consistently falling behind. Roland tried to work with the manager who was having problems. Being the kind and generous guy that Roland is, he spent too much time working with the guy without getting the problem solved. Two quarters of missed targets went by and guess what happened?"

"They both got sacked?"

"Of course. You know how it works. Shit flows downhill," said Michael.

"And that's how he ended up here?"

"That's right. He had good credentials and that was important to Golden Sunshine and their financiers. But I imagine he took a significant pay cut. And no more fancy office in a tower in Jo'burg. Instead he's out here swatting flies in the jungle with the rest of us."

On the way back to the office, Conner asked questions regarding the grade and tonnage reconciliations and Michael explained that everything they were mining seemed to balance with the plans. Conner requested copies of the monthly reports for the last year, so he could get a better understanding of the operation and perform his own checks and balances.

"I'll have copies made and ready for you tomorrow," said Michael as they drove climbed out of the truck in front of the office building.

Lyla and the Operation

Conner walked back across the yard to the Process Plant and asked one of the operators for directions to Lyla's office. He climbed the stairs to the second floor and spotted Lyla through the large window that looked out over the plant's interior.

She was working at her desk when Conner stuck his head in and said, "Is now a good time?"

Lyla's face lit up and she said, "Perfect, come on in and grab a chair. Would you like a coffee? I just made a fresh pot."

Conner noticed that Lyla's desk and in fact her entire office were immaculate. Clean and organized. She poured two cups and Conner said, "We didn't get much of a chance to talk last night."

"No, it almost seemed that Jenny planned the seating arrangements that way, so she could command your total attention," she laughed. "I think she quite fancies you."

"I got that impression too. I'll have to explain that the "Independent" in "Independent Engineer" precludes relations with the General Manager's wife. And besides, she's not my type."

"What is your type?" she teased.

"I'm not sure, but I'm pretty confident she's not it."

"Jenny is actually quite a remarkable person," said Lyla. "She devotes a lot of time and energy to volunteering at a clinic in Abengourou. It's called the Nouvel Espoir (New Hope) post-natal clinic." There is a high infant mortality rate in the Ivory coast. And because the hospitals are overcrowded, new mothers aren't given much time to recuperate nor the newborns monitored. They are released and sent back to their villages soon after the baby is born. Nouvel Espoir works with the hospital to identify patients that could use some more time to convalesce. She started the foundation which owns and operates the clinic that takes in mothers needing help with their newborns.

"That's admirable," said Conner. "Who pays for it?"

"Jenny solicited donations from local businesses and charities to buy an old rooming house and have it fixed up enough to use as the clinic. Now that it is operating, she gets grants from European and North American aid agencies for her operating budget. Golden Sunshine chips in too. It has room for twelve mothers that usually stay between two and five days. I give her a hand sometimes."

"Wow that is commendable. I'll bet the women she helps really appreciate her effort."

"Yes, it's heartwarming to see."

Setting the small talk aside, Lyla asked, "How can I help you with your assignment here?"

"Well, basically I'm here to check out the general health of the operation," Conner explained. "To see if there are any "red flags" that my client should be aware of before investing in the Company. You can help by running me through your plant, providing monthly operating statistics and pointing out where you see any problems or room for improvement which will, in effect, give my client additional upside when addressed."

"This plant is brand new and although I would have designed some things a bit differently, I have to say it runs extremely well. Why don't we take a walk around?"

They put on their hard hats and safety glasses and headed back outside. Lyla led Conner up a set of circular steel stairs to a catwalk like structure near the top of the plant. From their vantage point they could see the pit and crushing operation as well as the leach pad and solution ponds.

"After the ore is mined and crushed," she explained, "it is conveyed to the leach pad and deposited in long piles which are later leveled by a bulldozer. The leach drip lines, which are half inch perforated plastic tubing, are set on top of the crushed ore and "barren" cyanide solution, meaning it contains no gold, is distributed evenly over the pad. The solution percolates through the heap slowly dissolving the gold and the now "pregnant" solution flows along the bottom on the plastic liner into lined ditches and then into pregnant solution pond or "preg pond."

Lyla pointed out the ponds, three in total. The first two were completely covered with thousands of plastic balls, the size of grapefruit.

"What's with all the balls?" asked Conner.

"They keep the birds from landing in the ponds and drinking the cyanide solution. Most mining operations use nets to keep the birds off but sometimes the birds end up getting tangled in the nets. We find that balls, though more expensive, are better in the long run."

"The "pregnant" solution is pumped to the carbon columns," she said, "pointing to five large steel tanks. The tanks are filled with activated carbon and the solution is pumped to the highest tank. It flows by gravity down though the rest. The gold sticks to the carbon and the solution, no longer containing gold, flows out into the "barren" pond. It is then pumped back up onto the heap to repeat the cycle. A completely closed circuit, "zero discharge" system," she said quite proudly.

"What is the third pond for?" asked Conner pointing to the last pond which was the only empty one.

"That's the "storm" pond. Should we have a bad storm and there is too much rain for the ponds to handle, they are designed to overflow into each other and ultimately into the "storm" pond. That way no solution will ever be released into the environment."

"Let's go look at the strip circuit," Lyla directed.

They walked down the spiral stairs and around to the other side of the plant. The area was covered by a steel roof, but the sides were open. None-the-less it smelled quite strongly of ammonia.

"Here, the gold is removed, or "stripped" from the carbon by washing it with a hot caustic solution. After, the carbon is sent back to the columns to be used again. The strip solution is sent to the electro winning circuit where it is pumped into tanks and the gold is plated by electrolysis onto wire mesh. Later, once the wire mesh is laden with precipitate, it is washed off as a sludge. The sludge is melted in the furnace and the impurities come off with the slag. What we have left, and what is poured into the bricks is the "doré", about seventy percent gold and thirty percent silver. Would you like to see the Gold Room?"

"Lokossou Bamba showed it to me this morning. Quite impressive. And I saw the bags of sludge," Conner said. "But if you don't mind, I would like to go back to your office and have a look at some of the operating statistics."

They went back inside and up to the second floor where Lyla introduced Conner to the Plant Production Engineer, Mamadou Toungara. Mamadou's desk was in a larger work area outside Lyla's office. It was neat and organized and off to one side was a framed photo of a proud and happy looking Mamadou holding a young baby. Mamadou appeared to be about twenty-five and had a pleasant and sincere smile.

"Mamadou takes care of all the production statistics and generates the Process Plant operating reports," said Lyla. "He is a big help to me. Right now, he is working on a project to try and explain a discrepancy we see in the gold mass balance. Since my arrival six months ago, the gold produced has consistently been about five percent below the projections based on the feed solution analysis. Before that, insufficient records were maintained to do balances."

"We are pretty sure it is a mechanical error, like a problem with a scale or meter, because it is so consistent month to month," offered Mamadou. "It's frustrating that we can't make things balance. We must be overlooking something, but I don't know what."

"Perhaps we could sit down and review the data and your methodology. Are you available tomorrow?" Conner inquired.

"Certainly. I will have everything ready for you to look at. And if it's alright with you Miss Lyla, I'd like to work a little late tonight to check out a couple of ideas I have."

It was five o'clock and Konaté had left already so Conner rode back to the Chateau with Lyla.

"Mamadou seems keen to help," said Conner as Lyla drove the pick-up out the mine gate and accelerated down the gravel road. "How is he technically?"

"He doesn't have a lot of experience, but he is logical and not afraid to ask when he doesn't understand something. It is a real pleasure working with him."

The rain had just started again so Lyla turned on the windshield wipers and continued, "Mamadou has been here since the beginning. The engineering company that built the plant had their people commission it and stay on to get it running and train the operators. Because they hadn't hired a Plant Manager yet, Mamadou was left in charge for the first six months."

The rain was coming down harder now and Lyla slowed down and turned the windshield wipers on high as the truck splashed through the potholes.

"When they hired me, I became his boss and took over a lot of the responsibilities that had previously been his," Lyla continued. "For some people, that's a difficult transition. Having someone brought in above them. And for some guys, the fact that it's a woman can make things harder. But Mamadou welcomed me and has been nothing but helpful since day one. He's got a great attitude."

"It's nice to see a young guy eager to stay late to help," commented Conner.

"Yes, he's always been like that. But I try to discourage it unless necessary because he and his wife have a new baby and his help is probably required at home."

"So, what about the night life in Abengourou?" Conner asked as the downpour started to subside.

"There are a few bars and restaurants, pretty casual, a couple with entertainment occasionally," Lyla responded. "I don't get out that much in the evening."

"Then how about we venture out after dinner and find a place to have a beer?"

Lyla smiled and replied, "Sounds good to me. It's not often an Australian girl turns down a beer."

The Incident

They left the Chateau around eight o'clock and drove through town checking out a few places. It was Wednesday night and things were quiet. Most places were open air and they ended up stopping at a small bar/restaurant beside the river called the "Resto".

The owner brought them menus, but they explained that they were just stopping by for a beer. Conner was surprised when Lyla ordered a Guinness. He didn't expect bottles of Guinness to be available in such a remote location but was happy to follow suit. Lyla explained that Guinness was one of the most popular brands of beer in the country. They sat and chatted and enjoyed the beer and peaceful evening. There were a few other patrons, mostly watching a soccer game on the TV.

"So, tell me how you ended up in Abengourou?" Conner asked. "It's a hell of a long way from Australia."

She took a sip from her bottle and looked up toward ceiling for a second and said, "When I graduated from engineering, I went to work for the largest mining company in the country, at a huge iron ore mine in Western Australia. I had studied for four years and landed a great job with great pay and benefits. But I found that processing iron ore is only slightly more interesting than watching paint dry and it took me only a few months to re-alize that I was bored to tears. I couldn't imagine going through my career without enjoying the hell out of it. So, I split. I wanted a challenge. I wanted to learn. I wanted to live."

"Do you think you did the right thing?"

"I guess so. I miss home sometimes and my family all think I'm crazy. Perhaps I am. But at least I feel like I'm living, doing something I'm happy with. Not just a cog in a wheel." Her eyes lit up as she went on. "I went to Nevada first because I had heard about the developing mines and leading-edge technology. I ended up finding a job with a company that operated a couple of small heap leach gold operations near Beatty. I had a lot of responsibility and was able to learn tons about the technology in a short time. Met some interesting and colorful people. And in my spare time I got to visit places like Las Vegas, Reno, a lot of the little mining towns and even ski at Lake Tahoe. I was there a couple of years and then with that heap leach gold experience, I applied for this position as Process Plant Manager. It's a pretty good job for a twenty-eight-year-old."

Lyla seemed to be enjoying herself, getting out and having someone to talk to. Conner listened while she did most of the talking. She seemed to be enjoying the beer too, so he volunteered to be the driver on the way home and paced himself.

She told him about her family and growing up in Melbourne. Talked about some of the characters she met in Nevada. The time the mine was robbed when someone drove the Caterpillar loader through the wall of the process plant and gold room and took off into the desert with two gold bars. She talked about the places she'd like to visit in the future. The time flew by.

"I hope you don't mind me yakking so much," she said as they were on their way home. "I feel comfortable around you and it's been so long since I've had someone around that I could really talk to. I think I must have drunk too much."

"Not at all, I found your stories fascinating. It sounds like you've had some quite unique and exciting experiences."

"Next time I get to hear what makes you tick," she laughed.

They arrived back at the Chateau at around eleven o'clock where I was waiting for them and I told them Roland needed to talk to them about something terribly important.

I ran up to Roland's sitting room to inform him of their return.

Roland had nodded off, but I woke him, and he came downstairs.

"I have some bad news," he said while I waited to see if I would be needed anymore. "Mamadou Toungara, the Plant Production Engineer, is dead. His body was found a couple of hours ago at the bottom of the barren solution pond by one of the plant operators."

"That's terrible," said Lyla looking shocked. "What happened?"

"No one knows at this point. His body has been taken to the hospital morgue and his family has been notified."

"Is there something we should be doing tonight?" she asked.

"No, there is nothing more that can be done tonight. The security department will be launching a full investigation in the morning. I'm sorry to be the bearer of bad news."

Roland went to bed and I checked with Conner and Lyla to see if they needed anything.

They went upstairs and stopped at Lyla's door. She was badly shaken, and the effect of the Guinness was long gone.

"The poor guy. His poor wife and new baby. What a horrible thing to happen."

"Yes, a terrible shame," said Conner. He wrapped his arms around her and gave her a hug. We'll find out what happened tomorrow but tonight you should get some rest."

"Thanks Conner," she said. "I'd appreciate your help."

I retired to my bunk in the staff quarters and lay in the dark wondering what it was that made the Spirits decide to take Mamadou from his family.

Investigation

In the kitchen Wednesday morning, the staff were all talking about the drowning. The chef went about his regular morning routine baking baguettes and croissants but found time to add his opinions. After feeding the goat and monkey, I ate yesterday's bread and sipped a bowl of coffee mixed with hot milk while listening to the discussion. Nsia made sure things kept moving while people speculated on the reason for Mamadou's death. The consensus was that the Spirits had drowned Mamadou in a cyanide pond because of something Mamadou had done personally, or because he was helping the mining company steal their gold. Time would tell.

Konaté went to the mine early and met with Bamba.

"I got your message," said Konaté. "What the hell went on here last night?"

"Watch this," said Bamba. He played a video on his computer which showed one of the solution ponds in the dark. After a few seconds, two uniformed figures appeared dragging a body, sliding it into the pond and walking back in the direction from which they came. Then he turned it off.

"Were those your guys?" asked Konaté.

"Yes, the engineer showed up at a bad time. They didn't want him running off and telling everyone what was going on so one distracted him and the other hit him on the back of his head with the butt of his pistol. They called my radio and told me what happened. I told them to put him in the barren pond. Make it look like an accident."

"Why the barren pond?" asked Konaté.

"I thought it better to keep the attention away from the preg pond. They got sloppy. They should have been more careful making sure no one was watching. I replaced this video with a blank video and reported the camera being down."

"No other witnesses?"

Bamba shook his head.

"Good, then we'll just ride it out. Conduct a full investigation and conclude it was human error on the engineer's part," said Konaté as he got up to leave. "And Lokossou, make damn sure your people are more careful in the future," he added.

Michael arrived in the dining room just as Conner was finishing his breakfast. He had brought back a year's worth of Monthly Reports and presented them to Conner. "Some light reading for you mate," he said dropping the stack on the table.

"That should keep me out of trouble," Conner commented.

"Talking about trouble, I hear a chap drowned in one of the solution ponds last night. Nasty bit of business for Lyla."

"She'll be okay," said Conner. "But you're right. It's a shitty thing to have to deal with the aftermath of a fatality."

"Any idea what happened?" asked Michael looking for at least a morsel of information on which he could speculate and build a gossip worthy story."

"Not yet Michael. Keep you posted," said Conner as he picked up the bundle of reports and headed up to the library.

Halfway through the morning, Lyla returned from the mine and asked Conner if he would go to the hospital with her to talk to the coroner about the autopsy.

On the way to the hospital Lyla said, "I spoke to Bamba, who is conducting the investigation, but they haven't found too much. He says it appears that Mamadou slipped and fell into the pond and drowned. He said they had some security camera footage of Mamadou walking out there but it was dark, and they couldn't get a good picture. The one camera that was closest wasn't working. He asked me if I knew why he was out around the ponds that late in the evening. I told him I didn't have any idea."

"How was his body discovered?" asked Conner.

"A plant operator went out to check the pumps and noticed Mamadou's hard hat floating in with the bird balls. They had seen him around the plant that evening but couldn't find him anywhere, so they cleared away some of the balls and shone a light into the water and there was his body. They used the pole for moving the pump barges around to hook onto his clothing and pull his body out."

"Very strange," said Conner. You'd think he could have used the plastic balls for flotation while he called for help."

"Yes, that is strange," Lyla said as they pulled into the hospital parking lot. "And another strange thing is that one of his friends told me that he was a strong swimmer. It sounds to me like the cyanide must have got him."

The Abengourou hospital serviced a large part of the interior of the country and was therefore, huge and extremely busy. The largest in the country's interior, its footprint covered an area the size of several city blocks. It looked like it had been added on, again and again over the last fifty years. The outside was painted blue and white while the inside was mostly a greyish white. There were obvious signs of wear, missing ceiling tiles, worn floor paint, etc. The waiting room was full of people. Perhaps one hundred or more. Most of whom looked like they had been waiting a long time and were not at all well or happy. There were multiple hallways leading to various parts of the hospital and Conner and Lyla had no idea where to go.

They spotted a security guard and asked how to get to Dr, Kacou's office. The guard directed them to the receptionist's window where several people were already waiting. After standing in the line-up for a while, they realized that the woman behind the glass was helping people fill out forms when she wasn't being interrupted by the telephone and it was going to be quite some time before they reached the window.

Lyla walked up to the front of the line and said, "Excuse me, I just have a quick question…"

The receptionist, who was a big round woman with a big round hairdo to match, had a badge pinned to her ample bosom displaying the name "Rosie."

Before Lyla could finish her question, the telephone rang and obviously took priority. Lyla couldn't make out what was being said but the tone didn't sound business related. Every now and then Rosie would stifle a laugh making a noise not dissimilar to the air squeaking out of a balloon. When she hung up the phone, Rosie barked, "I'm sorry madam, unless you are gravely ill, which doesn't appear to be the case, you'll have to wait your turn just like these other people did. And the more I'm interrupted, the longer the process will take."

Lyla backed off and returned to stand with Conner in the line-up. She decided she wasn't in enough of a hurry to warrant getting into a fight with Rosie. The line moved slowly as Rosie instructed people on how to fill out the forms and answer other questions. Every few minutes the phone would ring and the whole process would grind to a halt. Eventually they reached the window and Rosie said, "Where are your forms? You can't be treated without completing the medical questionnaire and personal information forms."

"We're not here…" Lyla started as the phone suddenly rang. Rosie picked it up and spent the next few minutes dealing with the caller.

"Now, the forms?" she repeated.

"We're not here to be treated," said Lyla. "We just need directions to Dr. Kacou's office."

"You should have told me earlier. That's simple," replied Rosie. "There is a map on the wall around the corner," she said pointing to her left.

"Next time," said Lyla smiling.

"You should have told her earlier," joked Conner as they hurried around the corner.

Lyla answered Conner's quip with a dirty look.

They were glad to be out of the line-up and away from the waiting room and hoped they hadn't picked up any airborne germs.

When Lyla stepped into the office doorway she saw an older man with a bald head trimmed with curly white tufts of hair sitting behind a steel desk.

"Hello Dr. Kacou? I'm Lyla Townsend. We spoke on the phone."

Looking up, he used his forefinger to push his glasses up the bridge of his nose. As he rose to greet his guests, Lyle noticed that he was about a head shorter than her.

"Yes, please come in Miss Townsend. Nice to meet you. Sorry it couldn't have been under happier circumstances," Dr. Kacou said while shaking Lyla's hand.

"This is my friend and co-worker Conner Jackson," she motioned.

Shaking Conner's hand, "Please come in and sit down. Would you like some coffee or a glass of water?"

"No thanks," they both said while they sat down. Lyla had learned the hard way that it was best to drink only water from a bottle that you personally broke the seal on or beer from a bottle that you took the cap off if you didn't want to end up with a case of the "maux d'estomac".

"So, you're here about that young man that drowned last night?" inquired the doctor settling back in his chair and looking concerned.

"Yes, we are extremely interested in finding out what happened. Perhaps there is a way it can be prevented from happening again," said Conner.

"Okay, but first I must let you know that I am not a coroner. I'm a general surgeon. We don't currently have a coroner in Abengourou so we, the doctors in the hospital, take turns doing autopsies as required. That being said, the body showed signs consistent with drowning."

"So, you don't think it was because there was cyanide solution in the pond?" Lyla asked.

"Well, drowning and cyanide poisoning work in similar ways. They both starve the body of oxygen. So, it is possible that the cyanide might have speeded up the process. What cyanide concentration did the solution in the pond contain?"

"We usually maintain between one and two parts per million," answered Lyla.

"That is an extremely low concentration, it would require the victim to drink something around twenty liters to be fatal," he said as he did the calculation in his head. "Even if you consider what might be absorbed through the skin. A bigger influence on his death would have to be the fact that when he died he might have been unconscious. He had suffered a nasty bang on the back of his head."

Lyla and Conner looked at each other as they digested this news.

"How could that be?" Conner wondered aloud.

"It could have happened hours or minutes before death. Difficult to tell but it was recent. There was no blood because he was under water. I don't know if it was bad enough to render him unconscious, but I have ordered an x-ray which will give us a better idea. If the blow was strong enough, that would explain why he drowned. I can do an intracranial examination but prefer to do the x-ray first and see how things look without the trauma of opening the skull. Any ideas of what could have caused the blow?"

"Hard to say," said Lyla. "There are lots of things around the plant a person can bang their head on. That's why we wear hard hats. But out by the pond there isn't too much. Perhaps he slipped and fell hitting his head on the ground or a pipe."

"Well let's wait until we get the x-ray results back before we speculate too much," the doctor said pushing his glasses back up his nose again. "Anything else I can do for you?"

"No, I don't think so."

"I'll give you a call when I have something more. I'm hoping to get the x-ray done today but the machine is terribly busy and living patients have priority. Did you want to see the body?"

"Not really," answered Lyla getting up to go. "Thanks for your time Dr. Kacou. I'll wait for your call."

They walked back through the busy waiting area and returned to their truck.

On the way back to the Chateau Conner said, "This bang on the head thing is a bit troubling."

"What are you saying?"

"Just that it's troubling."

"Are you saying someone could have knocked him unconscious and dumped him in the pond?"

"It's a possibility. Though I have no idea why someone would do it. Robbery doesn't seem likely. Did he have any enemies?"

"Enemies? Mamadou? I doubt it. He was the nicest guy and friends with everyone," answered Lyla.

"Perhaps he was seeing someone else's wife on the side?"

"He'd be the last guy I would imagine doing that. Let's wait until we hear back from the doctor before we chase too many wild herrings."

"Perhaps I've read too many mystery novels, but it seems strange to me that he would say he was staying late because he had an idea of how he might solve the mystery of the missing gold and he winds up dead," Conner said.

"Now you've really gone off the deep end," she answered. "We don't even know if there is any missing gold. We just know it doesn't balance. It could be a simple instrumentation problem. I think you should find some new reading material."

"Ok, got it. Let's wait until we hear back from the doctor," Conner replied. "Now, in the interest of changing the subject, I really enjoyed our little outing last night," he smiled.

"Me too," Lyla responded and smiled back.

"How would you like to do it again Friday night, when things are a bit livelier in Abengourou? Perhaps start with dinner?"

"Sounds good to me. It will be nice to have a change from the Chateau menu."

"I don't head back to Abidjan until Sunday," he added, immediately wishing he hadn't.

"Oh," she said. She had briefly forgotten that he was on a short-term visit and found herself disappointed it wasn't longer term. They drove back to the Chateau in silence.

Conner went back to reviewing the Mine Reports in the library and Lyla went to meet with the young man they used to paint signs. She asked him to paint twenty more Danger/Poison signs to put around the ponds. Then she went to see Roland.

I was watering the potted plants in the hallway when Lyla arrived at Roland's office. I asked if either of them would like coffee or a cold bottle of water. They both wanted water, so I hurried down to the kitchen to get some.

"I went to see the coroner," said Lyla. "I just wanted to fill you and Adjobi in, but he isn't in his office. I left a note on his desk. Do you have a minute?"

"Certainly. Please go ahead."

"Actually, he's not a coroner, he's a surgeon, but the doctors at the hospital take turns doing autopsies. I was amazed by how much he knew about cyanide poisoning for someone not normally involved with it."

"You'd be surprised," answered Roland. "There are quite a few cyanide poisonings in African countries."

"How's that," questioned Lyla.

"It is because there is a high concentration of cyanide in the skin of the cassava root. Cassava is a staple in most tropical African countries. The cyanide is stable in the skin, which is not eaten, but if the skin happens to be burned, cyanide gas is released, and it can be quite toxic. Seldom fatal but in an enclosed area, bad enough to make someone extremely ill."

"It's a good thing I'm not cooking. I'd probably kill everyone in the Chateau," she said attempting to lighten the mood.

I arrived with the water bottles and went back to my chores.

"Anyway," Lyla continued, "he said the cause of death was drowning, not cyanide poisoning. But he did mention that Mamadou had a nasty bump on the back of his head. He's ordered an x-ray to determine if it was bad enough to render him unconscious."

Just then Konaté strode down the hall and into Roland's office. I wanted to keep away from him but also wanted to be polite. I stuck my head around the corner of the doorway as he was sitting down with his back to me. I caught Roland's attention and pointed at Konaté. Roland asked if he would like some water and he flatly said no. I went back to my work but could hear most of what was going on. Especially from Konaté.

Konaté sat back in his chair gazing at the ceiling and played with his big gold rings while Roland filled him in on what Lyla had related. When he got to the part about the bang on Mamadou's head, Konaté said, "What difference does it make? That stupid man. He probably slipped on the wet plastic liner and smacked his head on something. He shouldn't have been out there in the dark. He shouldn't have been out there by himself. What was he doing anyway?" he looked angrily at Lyla.

"I have no idea," she answered.

"Well you should have an idea what your staff are doing don't you think? And you should make certain that they know how to work safely. Then this type of thing wouldn't happen, would it? Now we have a big goddamn mess on our hands."

Lyla was upset, and Roland interrupted, "Now calm down Adjobi, you know it wasn't Lyla's fault. She's just trying to find out what happened like the rest of us, so we can prevent it from happening again."

"Well she can prevent it from happening again by making sure her staff are not wandering around the ponds in the dark ever again. Is that too much to ask?" he said getting up from his chair and pointing his finger at Lyla.

"You know the operators need to check the pumps," Lyla protested, anger surging through her veins.

"Yes, but I don't need any goddamn pencil pushing engineers roaming around aimlessly in the night, and getting themselves killed," he said as he turned and left the office.

Lyla rolled her eyes and Roland told her not to worry about Adjobi. "He's under a lot of pressure and tends to overreact."

"Yeah? Well I don't need that kind of crap from a loudmouth sack of kangaroo shit like him," Lyla said as she also got up and left.

Roland reached for his bottle. I went for ice.

Missing Gold

Lyla returned to the mine and Conner spent the remainder of the day reviewing and checking the mine data in his makeshift office in the library. The average grade of the deposit was around one gram of gold per tonne of rock. The mine plan for the last year had them mining in an area of higher grade, estimated at 1.2 g/t. The actual production records from sampling the production drill holes and the belt samplers of the crushing facility incorporating thousands of assays returned a slightly higher grade. And the reported tonnage from the crusher belt scales corresponded well with the survey volume reconciliations. The mining equipment seemed to be in good shape and had good mechanical availability rates. There didn't appear to be any geotechnical problems. All in all, the mining operation seemed to be going well with no major concerns. That would make the investment bankers happy.

Conner, Lyla and Michael ate dinner that night in the staff dining room. The chef had made braised rabbit in red wine gravy with boiled cassava. I was serving and stuck close so I could listen quietly to their stories. Their lives were intriguing to me. I could have listened for hours, and as you have probably noticed by now, sometimes did.

Conner remarked on how delicious the dinner was and everyone agreed. Then he asked Michael how he ended up at Abengourou.

"My wife's a nurse at a busy hospital in Johannesburg and works all the shifts. Days, nights and afternoons. She works like mad for four weeks and gets a week off. At my previous job, I worked nine to five, Monday to Friday. I hardly ever saw her. She was either at work or sleeping. Except on her days off, and then I was usually at the office all day."

Michael paused to ask the others if anyone wanted the last piece of rabbit on the platter and they all declined politely knowing that he had his sights set on it. Michael promptly speared it with his fork and stuffed it in his mouth.

"That must have been tough on your relationship," commented Lyla.

"Indeed," said Michael, chewing and swallowing the last morsel. Wiping the gravy off his chin with a napkin he continued, "And she loves her work and didn't want to change jobs. So, I did. Now I work the same schedule as she does. Four weeks on and a week off."

"And how is that working out?" asked Conner.

"Splendidly. Sometimes I return to Jo'burg, but we usually meet somewhere for a little holiday on our breaks." Michael wiped up the last of his gravy from his plate with the end of a baguette. "Last month we met in Crete and later this month we are visiting the Azores. It's like a honeymoon every four weeks," Michael said showing his piano-like grin.

After dinner they all went to the games room. Michael watched recorded episodes of "Cheers" from VHS tapes on the TV and laughed loudly as Cliff Clavin explained that alcohol selectively kills off the weaker brain cells which is why people always feel smarter after they've had a couple of beers. The antics of Sam and Diane and the rest of the group at the Cheers bar continued in the background while Conner and Lyla played a few games of pool. While they played, Lyla asked Conner questions about his background.

Conner explained that he grew up in Bancroft Ontario where his father worked in a uranium mine. That's what first sparked his interest in mining and inspired him to go into engineering. After high school he went to university in Kingston, which was not too far from Bancroft. He had a brother who was now a pilot for Air Canada and a sister who lived in Oakville, near Toronto. Although she had a degree in psychology, his sister devoted her time to raising Conner's three nephews.

"Are your siblings older or younger than you?" asked Lyla.

"Both younger. My sister's the baby and the only one that's married. My brother is on his own, divorced like me. He lives North of Toronto. Not too far from the airport.

Lyla was surprised to hear that Conner had been married at one time.

"It was right after we finished school," said Conner. "We met during third year, fell in love and married right after graduation. We started our life together in a small town in the Yukon. I worked at a zinc mine and she worked for the Territorial Government as a social worker. It didn't take long and we started having problems. She was unhappy and said she wanted to leave the Yukon. I offered to quit my job so we could find somewhere that better suited her. But it turned out she wasn't just sick of the Yukon. She'd had enough of me too."

"That' awful," said Lyla. "It must have been hard on you."

"Sure, I was devastated at first. But then I realized it was good that she broke it off. Although we seemed to be so much in love in the beginning, it turned out that we didn't really have much in common. We were so young. We actually had the marriage annulled and went our separate ways."

Conner finished cleaning off the table and racked up the balls for another game. He motioned for Lyla to go ahead while he continued his story.

"Anyway, being free from responsibility again, I returned to school to do my master's degree and party some more. Been working as an independent ever since. No boss. No headaches. Low overhead. I eat what I kill. Last year I was able to take two months off. I chartered a boat and sailed single handed around the Caribbean. Anchored in a different harbor or bay every night."

"Sounds like a great holiday. Didn't you get lonely?"

"Not really. I did meet other people cruising and we'd run into each other from time to time. I guess I've just gotten used to being on my own."

"I love sailing," said Lyla. "My family had a boat when I grew up in Melbourne. I was into racing in a big way."

"Well next time we'll have to go cruising together and share the cost of the charter."

"Now you're talking. And scuba diving. I understand the Caribbean has outstanding coral reefs."

"The reefs off Belize and Honduras are incredible. They're said to be the best outside of the Great Barrier Reef," added Conner. "You're a diver too?"

They played more pool and talked through the evening discovering they had quite a few common interests and enjoying each other's company.

The next morning Conner fed the goat and monkey with me and ate breakfast with Michael while Lyla went for her run. Conner and Lyla drove to the mine together where they spent a good part of the morning going through the plant reports and calculating the amount of gold lost in the system.

Meanwhile, back at the Chateau, Roland was nursing his hangover and trying to decide how he could approach Konaté and get him to lighten up on Lyla. He liked Lyla and considered her a solid asset for the operation. The last thing he wanted was to lose her because Konaté was so outspoken and downright rude. Finally, he decided to go and talk to Konaté in his office.

"Good morning Adjobi," said Roland from the doorway.

"Morning Roland, please come in. How can I help you?"

"It's about Lyla," said Roland sitting down and running his fingers through his thin hair. "You see, I'm quite fond of her and feel that in spite of her limited experience, she's doing a pretty good job at running the plant."

"I agree," said Konaté.

"It's just that," Roland paused, "you were a bit hard on her yesterday. She was quite shaken up after you left my office."

"She's a big girl. She'll get over it," said Konaté.

"I'm not sure I like that attitude. I'm asking you to treat her more courteously."

Konaté thought a moment and got up and closed the door. He sat back down, looked at Roland and said, "You don't get it do you?"

"Get what?" asked Roland.

"Roland, do we want people snooping around the solution ponds?"

Before Roland had a chance to answer, Konaté said, "Of course not. And it's up to me to discourage them. I told you I would handle the situation and that's what I'm doing. It's fine for you to be warm and fuzzy, but someone must keep things from going off the rails here. I don't care if they think I'm a prick. I'm sure I've been called a lot worse. But I'm not here to make friends. I'm here to get a job done. And if being a bit of a shit to "Sweet Miss Lyla" keeps her away from the ponds, that works for me."

I saw Roland returning to his office looking frustrated. He spent the next couple of hours staring out the window and then told me it was time for a piano lesson.

Conner and Lyla checked the calculations and confirmed that the gold balance was indeed off by 5%. They made a list of the possible causes for the discrepancy. They included a leak in pond or pad, some organic material in heap that the gold could be deposited on, a faulty flow meter in a pipe, inaccurate gold concentration analysis in the lab, a problem with the weighing or sampling of the gold bars or a combination of any of the above.

Then they addressed each possibility one by one. The ponds all had double liners with leak detection systems. If there was solution breaching the top liner, there was a collection area in the lowest spot with a sampling port. All the ponds were checked, and no solution found between the liners.

The pad actually had 3 liners. Two plastic liners with a clay liner below. With millions of tonnes of crushed ore stacked on the pad it was impossible to see if the liner had been damaged but if there was a leak in the upper liner, the solution would flow by gravity between the two liners to the detection port. If both liners were ruptured, the solution would make the clay wet, which in turn would cause it to swell, which would seal off the leak. If the clay didn't seal the leak and the cyanide solution entered the groundwater system, it would be detected in the array of groundwater monitoring wells surrounding the pad.

No sign of leaks. No cyanide in the wells.

The ore was crushed to 5/8 inch and was beautifully clean. No wood, no organics. They spoke with geologist to see if there was a possibility of some carbonaceous mineral in the ore. He confirmed that there was nothing but nice clean igneous rock.

There was a flow meter in the pipe coming from the pregnant solution pond to the carbon columns. Flow meters are generally accurate but there was a spare in the warehouse, so Lyla decided to have it installed in series with the other as a check.

The solutions were analyzed in the lab with an atomic adsorption (AA) machine. The AA machine results were not suspect because they have standards for control and calibration. Standards were samples of solution containing a known concentration of gold. Lyla instructed the Chief Assayer to order a new set of standards from the commercial lab in Abidjan just to be sure.

They ruled out operator error because measurement is straight forward. The machine does everything and measures accurately to .01 parts per million (ppm). Pregnant solution contained around 1.5 ppm of gold and the barren solution was about 0.5 ppm. The difference is 1.0 ppm and measuring to .01 ppm would therefore give an accuracy of 1%.

They thought about a possible problem with the scales used to weigh the gold bars but thought that unlikely because the weights reported by the refiner matched those of the mine. And the purity was checked by a third-party referee and the analysis almost always came back spot on. Also, any slag left over from the weekly pour was collected and stored in the vault until next week when it is added to the following pour.

It was getting late in the afternoon. "We must be overlooking something," Conner said rubbing his head. "Five percent is a lot of gold. With a production rate of 200,000 oz. per year, that is 10,000 oz. About $3.5 million."

"I know," said Lyla. "I'm surprised Konaté isn't ragging on me about it. He sure got worked up yesterday."

"Oh, is that right? What did he say?"

"He said to make sure my staff is not wandering around the ponds in the dark ever again. It sounded like he was trying to blame me for what happened to Mamadou."

"What an asshole," said Conner in disgust. "I think it makes him feel good to put other people down."

"I don't know why Roland puts up with him," Lyla added.

They drove back to the Chateau together speculating on what Mamadou could have been thinking of when he said he wanted "to check out a couple of ideas he had."

Lyla had not heard back from the doctor so when she reached the Chateau she went to call the hospital.

Conner wanted to chat with Roland and found him in his sitting room. Roland was having a whiskey and offered one to Conner which he gladly accepted.

"So how is your due diligence coming?" Roland asked as they sat down.

"Very well. Still trying to work out some bugs in the Plant mass balance but from what I've seen so far, everything seems fine."

"Glad to hear it. And everyone being helpful?"

"Yes, most definitely. They have all been extremely cooperative. They are awfully proud of the operation and their individual departments. It's nice to see."

"And your comments are nice to hear."

"I was particularly impressed by the level of security. Sixteen staff and I've never seen a video monitoring system as extensive as that," said Conner swirling his ice around in the whiskey. "How did you end up contracting that firm?"

"Originally, we had planned to have our own security staff, but we got quite a reasonable quote from them and thought we would give it a try. You see, it was just as we were starting up and we were incredibly stretched for manpower. The Company is owned by the Major General of the Ivorian army who is Adjobi Konaté's brother-in-law, so we had a connection."

"Nice to have a Major General's salary and a security company making you money on the side."

Roland got up to pour himself another drink. Conner was still working on his.

"General Tiémoko is a pretty amazing man. He's only forty-five and he's made his way to the top of the armed forces. Incredibly ambitious and tremendously successful in whatever he does. He's also well connected. His uncle was the President of the country before the current one so people give him a lot of consideration."

"Sounds like quite a guy," commented Conner.

"They say he sleeps only four hours a day and works or reads twenty hours. And interesting to talk to. He's knowledgeable on so many subjects and current events. He's also quite generous and has personally donated a significant amount of money to Jenny's clinic."

"So, if he's only forty-five and reached the top of the military ladder, what does he do now?" asked Conner.

"That's a good question. Because a man with his level of ambition is not going to suddenly stop. If I were the Minister of Defense, I'd be worried about holding on to my job," laughed Roland draining his glass.

Lyla managed to get through to the reception desk at the hospital.

"Abengourou Hospital, Rosie speaking. How may I help you?" said the voice.

"Just my luck," thought Lyla. "May I please speak to Dr. Kacou?"

"I'm sorry, Dr. Kacou is not available right now. He's away from the hospital."

"When will he be back?"

"I don't know. He went to Abidjan."

"Is there some way for me to get in touch with him. It's actually quite important," said Lyla.

"If it's an emergency medical issue I can put you through to another doctor."

"I'm looking for some information about an autopsy he performed the other day."

"If the patient is already dead, it doesn't sound like an emergency," replied Rosie. "Please call back tomorrow," she added as she hung up.

The General

Friday morning Lyla organized her maintenance crew to install the spare flow meter in the main feed line. It meant shutting down the plant for a couple of hours which in turn would mean lost production. She should have notified her direct boss, Konaté, but was still too angry to talk to him. And besides, she was afraid he would tell her not to bother installing the second meter. She would bury the interruption under routine maintenance. It would take about twenty-four hours of operation to have enough data to determine if there was a discrepancy between the meters.

Conner spent the morning with the geologist reviewing the ongoing exploration drilling program and the mine plans for the future. When he finished, he went back to the plant where he and Lyla re-checked their calculations regarding the gold balance once more.

When they were leaving to go home, they could see activity over at the security barracks. There were a couple of military jeeps and several uniformed soldiers saluting someone.

"I wonder what that's all about," said Conner.

"Probably the General. He visits a couple of times a month. Usually on a Friday. Stays at the Chateau overnight. Roland wines and dines him and Jenny falls all over him. It's quite an arse kissing show."

"Sounds like a good night for us to be going out," said Conner. "It is indeed," smiled Lyla.

They arrived back at the Chateau shortly before six and made plans to leave an hour later. When Conner came back downstairs, the General was just walking in the front door. Roland was there to welcome the General and I was there to carry his overnight bag to his room.

Roland spotted Conner and introduced the two. "Conner, I'd like you to meet Major General Tiémoko. He is here to check up on his security team." They shook hands and Roland continued, "Conner is the Independent Engineer of the underwriter that is financing the mine's expansion program."

The General was tall and fit looking. He was dressed in civilian clothes but had a military aura about him, the way he held himself, even the way he spoke. He came across as the kind of person that people either feared or sought approval from.

They shook hands and Tiémoko looked deeply into Conner's eyes. It was as if he was saying, "I'm suspicious of you and I know you're up to something."

"I trust you are finding everything in order," commented the General.

"Oh yes, Roland runs a top-notch operation. One of the best I have ever seen."

"And his wine cellar is one of the best I have seen," replied the General. "He is an excellent host."

Conner looked up to see Lyla coming down the stairs. She looked terrific. All dressed up with her hair down.

Tiémoko also did a double take and said, "Miss Townsend, what a nice surprise. You get lovelier each time I see you."

He took her hand and kissed her on both cheeks and stood back to look at her up and down. Lyla couldn't help but blush.

"My my," he said. "Now I remember what I really like about visiting the Chateau. I hope you'll be joining us for dinner."

Just then Jenny swooped in and the General greeted her with kisses as well.

"Unfortunately, Lyla will not be dining with us this time," said Jenny. Then turning to Lyla, Jenny smiled and added, "But you must join us in the future my dear."

Jenny took the General by the arm and led him off to the pool patio with Roland following behind. Conner and Lyla left through the front door.

"My goodness," said Conner. "You certainly do look nice? What a beautiful dress."

"Thanks, it's new," said Lyla beaming. "I don't get out that often, so I haven't had a chance to wear it yet."

"Well, you're going to be turning some heads tonight.

They drove downtown to a restaurant on the main street which they had been told had a reputation of serving the best food in town.

It was big and busy. There was a band setting up in the back corner on a small stage surrounded by a dance floor. A hostess led them to a table near the dance floor and gave them menus.

They ordered beers and the mixed barbeque platter to share. It had been a busy week and there was a lot to talk about. When the meal arrived, they were surprised to see how huge it was. It came on a sizzling grill atop a fire box housing white hot charcoal. While they ate, they both told funny stories about their past and laughed. Each talked about what they would like to do in the future. After dinner they danced. Lyla looked terrific in her new dress and caught everyone's attention. The subject that Conner would be leaving the day after tomorrow was avoided.

The music had finished and most of the restaurant guests were already gone by the time they left and returned to the Chateau.

I was still cleaning up after the dinner when they arrived. Roland and Jenny had gone to bed and Konaté, who had also come for dinner, and the General were in the drawing room drinking brandy. Roland had asked me to stick around in case they needed something.

I met Conner and Lyla at the front door and asked if I could get them anything. They thanked me but said no and headed upstairs. I went to help Nsia finish cleaning up.

At the door to her room Lyla turned to Conner and asked, "Would you like to come in?"

"Yes, I would," answered Conner.

Why did the Spirits made me hear that?

Once I was finished in the kitchen, I waited in the hallway for a while, probably until around midnight and briefly nodded off to sleep. When I awoke, I could no longer hear the muffled voices. Thinking that they might have gone to bed, I went to peek through the crack in the drawing room door. When I got there, I heard low voices and stopped for a second to listen.

"...plan to have him killed so I can take control of the government," said the voice of the General.

I hurried quickly back down the hall to my chair and stayed there until they finished.

"Why did the Spirits made me hear that? What did it mean and what did they want me to do with the information?" I was in an awful predicament. I felt sick. "Why had the Spirits picked me? What should I do about it? What could I do?"

I tossed in my bunk for most of the night and fell asleep just before dawn with nightmares of Spirits pointing at me and calling my name. When I awoke, it turned out that Nsia was the one calling me.

"What are you doing still in bed?" barked Nsia. "We need to serve breakfast. The General's returning to Abidjan and always leaves at nine sharp."

I helped serve breakfast to Roland and the General. Jenny was sleeping in. The General left and Roland went to his office. I considered telling him what I heard last night but what could he do? Confront the General? He and the General seemed too close. I would need to tell him I was eavesdropping and heard him say it. At the very least, it would upset him, and Roland didn't need any more aggravation. I decided to leave Roland alone for now.

What did those words mean anyway? It sounded like there was a plan to kill someone. The President? I hadn't heard him say the President. Perhaps I heard things incorrectly? I decided I needed to talk to my father.

"Nsia, I'm not feeling well. Do you mind if I go home?" I asked.

"That's fine Kwame. You've been a big help. We can handle things here. Come back Monday morning."

I walked back into Abengourou to catch the bus from the main terminal to my village and noticed the General's jeep parked out front of a commercial center. The sign advertised "Currency Exchange". The driver was waiting by the car. I hurried to catch my bus.

When I arrived at my village I found my father. He was with the elders but left the group to talk with me.

After explaining to him what I overheard he asked, "Have you told anyone else?" looking serious and a bit annoyed.

"No, no one."

"Well don't. This isn't your business. You shouldn't have been listening in the first place."

"What if he means to harm the President?"

"The President and the General are both powerful men. Perhaps they will struggle for political control of this country. But it is not up to you to decide who is right and who is wrong. What happens is out of our hands. It is the will of the Spirits. Interfering will only get you in trouble. I don't want to hear any more about it."

I understood what my father was saying but continued feeling that something should be done. If this conflict was indeed the will of the Spirits, there must be some reason why they had let me overhear the plans.

Visit to My Village

Conner and Lyla woke late and lay in bed talking and listening to the multitude of birds singing and chirping outside Lyla's bedroom window. The sun was shining, and neither were in a hurry to go anywhere.

"You're a woman of many talents" kidded Conner. "Last night was wonderful."

"Never underestimate a girl from "down-under," " Lyla replied.

Hunger finally got the better of them and they went downstairs for a late breakfast. When they finished, Lyla called the doctor again to inquire about the x-ray results. This time he was in his office.

"Actually, there was no x-ray. I was called away for a family emergency in Abidjan and didn't get back until late yesterday. By that time, they had cremated the body," said Dr. Kacou.

"How could that be?" asked Lyla somewhat shocked.

"I don't know. They should have obtained my signature on the death certificate prior to doing the cremation. But it is customary to either bury or cremate the body after the third day, which was Friday."

"So, there was no signed death certificate?"

"Actually, there was, but the signature was illegible. I have no idea who signed it," answered Kacou. "Cause of death, "Accidental Drowning.""

"So, we will never know if he was conscious when he went in the pond?"

"I'm sorry, no. But remember, even after completing the autopsy, it would still have been a guess."

"I understand," said Lyla. "Sorry to hear you had a family emergency. I hope everything is ok."

"That's the other thing that's bothering me. I was given a note that said my mother had been admitted to the hospital in Abidjan and was gravely ill. It turned out to be completely wrong. My mother was at home feeling fine. The note was likely meant for someone else or I am the victim of a sick joke. Either way, it was odd."

Lyla told Conner about her conversation with the Kacou.

"Perhaps someone didn't want Kacou to finish the autopsy."

"Do you think we should pass that info on to Roland and Konaté?"

"Let's keep our cards close to our chests for a bit," said Conner. "How about we take a drive?"

"Where to?"

"I'd like to check the new flow meter and see if it is registering the same volume as the old one. I'm hoping its five percent off and our gold balance problem will be solved."

"Back to the mine? Why not? I wasn't looking forward to a day off anyway," she said facetiously.

They took Lyla's pick-up and Conner drove.

"Do you still think I've gone off the deep end?" Conner asked. "Aren't you a bit suspicious about foul play?"

"I guess we shouldn't rule it out."

"I feel like we should be extremely careful about what we say and to whom," said Conner. "We don't want to end up like Mamadou because we stuck our noses where they weren't wanted."

"I agree," said Lyla. "Our job is to worry about the technical and operational aspects of the mine. We are not getting paid to oversee the project security."

"The problem is that we can't do the technical part of our job properly if we don't know what's going on."

"And we can't do it at all if we get ourselves killed," answered Lyla. "Let's see what the meter says before we get too carried away with speculation."

As they passed through the village near the mine they noticed a group of young men on the soccer field. One of them waved and came running up to their truck. It was me.

"Miss Lyla, Conner, welcome to my village. Do you have time to stop? I would like to introduce you to my family."

Conner looked at Lyla and she said, "We would love to meet your family."

I pointed out my family's house and they went and parked on the gravel road in front of it. I led them into the yard which was canopied by several large trees. I called to my mother who was inside the house.

My mother emerged from the house wiping her hands on her apron. She was a beautiful woman, tall, perfect posture and hair cut so short that it accentuated her fine features. She was probably wishing she had had some advanced warning about having company but was far too polite to show anything but warm hospitality. There were children everywhere. My twelve-year-old sister was carrying my one-year-old brother around on her hip. The six and eight-year-old were chasing a piglet around the yard. There were dogs and chickens and the nine and fourteen-year-old came around the corner pulling a rope that turned out to have a goat on the other end. Only my father, who was taking care of the village business with the elders, was absent.

"Welcome to our home. Come and sit down. What can I get you? Would you like lunch?" asked my mother after I had introduced them.

"No, thank you," Lyla replied. "We just finished breakfast. Kwame invited us to meet his family and we didn't want to miss the opportunity. He is extremely proud of you."

"Come and meet my brothers and sisters," I said and introduced them to each one. It was easy to see, the young ones especially, were terribly excited to have white people or at least outsiders as company in their home.

We all talked a while. Conner and Lyla asked the children questions about their school and the games they played. The children also asked questions. "What does it feel like to have blue eyes?" my sister asked Lyla? "Does it make things look blue?" We all laughed about that one.

After a while I said, "My friends and I are looking for two more players for a game of soccer. Will you help us out for a bit?"

"I'm afraid I don't have proper shoes," said Lyla pointing to her hiking boots.

"That doesn't matter," I said. "Most of us play in bare feet. It will just be for fun."

Conner and Lyla agreed and we all headed over to the soccer field. Including the rest of the children who wanted to watch. Only my mother didn't come, and I had a feeling I knew why. As we were leaving, I saw her pick up a chicken and walk around the side of the house.

Conner and Lyla were on opposite teams and it was a terrific match. Everyone, none-the-least Conner, were amazed at how fast Lyla could run. We played for over an hour, until everyone was exhausted. Conner considered quitting earlier, but his team mates wouldn't hear of it. Not to mention the crowd of cheering onlookers that had gathered on the sidelines. Lyla's team won 3-0.

Conner and Lyla were heading back to their car when my mother emerged from the house and waved for them to come in. She said she had dinner cooking and wanted them to stay.

"You must stay," she said. "It would mean a lot to us. And we have plenty of food."

The pair were sweaty from the soccer game and agreed to join them for dinner as long as there was time to go back to the Chateau and get changed first.

When they returned, I took them over to the animal rehabilitation facility at the Sanctuaire de Faune de l 'or and asked the vet if I could introduce them to Okwan. The vet was proud of his facility and happy to have visitors. Okwan's leg was almost healed he looked great. He was well fed and muscular and it was easy to tell he was happy to see me. He came strolling over when he heard me call his name. My mother had given me the parts of the chicken she wasn't using for dinner wrapped up in a breadfruit leaf. I put them in Okwan's food tray and he devoured them.

"What a magnificent animal" said Lyla. What do you plan to do with him once he has recovered?

"We would like to release him into the sanctuary but will need to find a female as well," answered the vet. "We have our name on the waiting lists of several game reserves. They often find they have too many of a certain species and must reduce the numbers. They would much rather give them to other sanctuaries or even a zoo than cull them."

We went back to find that my father had arrived home.

I introduced Lyla and Conner and he welcomed them to our home. Conner gave my father a bottle of wine he'd picked up in town as well as a bottle of maple syrup he'd brought with him from Canada.

"I hope Kwame isn't interrupting your free time by making you join us," said my father.

"No Piesie, on the contrary. This is the highlight of our week," answered Lyla. "This is Conner's last night here and we consider ourselves honored to be able to spend it with you and your wonderful family."

We all sat down and my mother served a wonderful dinner of stewed chicken with tomatoes and vegetables with white rice. Conner opened the wine with the corkscrew on his Swiss Army knife and my father and the other adults shared it. But not before my father shared some with the Spirits. After dinner I played the dondo and everyone sang along.

When they finally left, after many goodbyes and promises to visit again, Conner and Lyla decided to continue to the mine to check out the flow meter. It was still early and there was no hurry to get back to the Chateau."

They drove to the mine, parked the pick-up and went inside the Process Plant building. Lyla retrieved her notebook from her office where she had recorded the meter readings Friday morning. They went downstairs to the main pipeline delivering solution from the preg pond to the carbon columns and recorded the numbers from both meters again. After subtracting Friday's values, the two numbers were almost identical. The meter was not the problem.

Conner said, "I'm wondering if we might be able to see something around the ponds at night that we didn't see during the day."

"What do you mean?" asked Lyla?

"I'm thinking about what happened to Mamadou. His body was found around nine o'clock at night. Its eight now. Perhaps it was a recurring event. Let's check out the ponds."

"I don't know Conner. It's dark and I wouldn't want to piss Konaté off. He specifically said he didn't want anyone out there in the dark. Remember the security cameras."

"Fuck Konaté."

"I know," said Lyla. "But why let him know that we're checking out the ponds at night. We'd be playing into his hand. It would be better to do it without anyone being aware."

Conner thought about it and agreed. Though he would have preferred to have gone out in plain sight of the cameras just to spite Konaté.

They found that they had a clear view of all the ponds from the carbon storage shed behind the plant, yet it was secluded enough for them not to be seen. It was a beautiful clear night and the bright moon made it easy for them see once their eyes had become accustomed. The carbon was stored in one tonne tote sacks and they climbed up and sat on one to watch and wait. They waited for about half an hour and nothing happened. The mosquitos were becoming an annoyance and Lyla was quickly losing patience when suddenly, a section of the perimeter fence between the preg pond and the security barracks was pushed up and two figures wearing camouflaged army fatigues made their way through.

The Discovery

Lyla gasped, and Conner put his hand on her wrist and his finger up to his lips. They slid down of the sack and pulled back farther into the shadows, but they could still see what the intruders were doing.

One of them shone a flashlight around the pond enclosure presumably looking for any sign of witnesses. Finding no one, they dragged two burlap sacks through the opening in the fence and left them near the edge of the pond. The one with the light shone it at the bird balls in the corner of the preg pond and his partner used a hooked pole to pull one of the balls over to the side and up on to the liner. It was attached to a thin line that was tied to a thicker rope which the two pulled until a sack emerged from the pond. Then they repeated the process retrieving another sack. Having both sacks out of the water and on the flat ground, they untied them and attached the new sacks to the ropes slipping them into the pond. They hauled the recovered sacks through the fence, pulled it closed and disappeared into the night.

"What do you think is in the sacks?" whispered Lyla.

"My guess would be activated carbon."

"They're stealing gold by loading it onto the carbon from the pregnant solution? Do you think that's what got Mamadou killed?"

"That would be my guess," answered Conner.

Conner and Lyla waited a few moments to make sure no one was watching and hurried back to their pick-up.

"Those guys most likely work for the security company and are following orders so there isn't much point reporting this to the Security Manager." said Lyla as she maneuvered the pick-up out of the parking area.

"I don't think so. That would make us witnesses and until we have a better idea what's going on, who's doing it and who we can or can't trust, we're better off keeping it to ourselves."

On their way back to the Chateau, they discussed their options. Lyla drove slowly because it was pitch dark and pedestrians walking along the side of the road were hidden in the darkness.

"It seems to me," said Conner, "it's got to be one of two scenarios. Either everyone at the mine is innocent and an outsider is stealing the gold, or it is an inside job."

"Let's assume it's the first scenario. That everyone involved with the mine is completely innocent," speculated Conner. "There's an outsider stealing the gold. We tell security, they play back the tapes, the thieves are identified and apprehended. Problem solved."

"Right," replied Lyla. "Except what are the chances of that? They came through the fence right next to the security barracks, wearing camouflage uniforms. So, they are most likely military. The army runs the security for the operation. The Operations Manager is the General's brother-in-law and the General Manager may even be party to the whole thing as well. I'd bet we're looking at scenario two."

"And if it is an inside job, instead of the thieves being identified and apprehended, we just open a big can of worms. A bogus investigation like the last one that likely involved erasing tapes and prematurely cremating the evidence."

"Well we can't just ignore it," responded Lyla. "We have to do something."

"You're right," replied Conner. "But we have to make sure we do it in a way that doesn't get us killed like Mamadou. Do you have any ideas?" Conner asked as they pulled up and parked in front of the Chateau.

Lyla looked at Conner and said with a smile, "I really think the best thing would be for us to sleep on it."

"Excellent idea!" replied Conner as they headed upstairs.

When Conner awoke, light was streaming through the window and Lyla was awake and watching him.

"Good morning," said Lyla. "I thought you might sleep all day."

"How long have you been watching me?"

"A while. I wanted to tell you it worked."

"What worked?" he asked rubbing his eyes.

"Sleeping on it. I have an idea."

"Let's hear it," said Conner rubbing his eyes.

"It's actually quite simple. We wait until Monday morning when there are lots of people at the mine and I do my routine walk around the ponds. I pretend to notice something odd near the ball with the string. I call a plant operator over and he fishes around until we find the rope and the sack and call security. They can investigate and conclude whatever they want but at least we'll have put an end to the stealing in a public way that doesn't endanger ourselves."

"That would work," said Conner. "But what would stop them from doing it again?"

"I could institute a program of checking the ponds daily for any foreign objects. The only drawback I see," said Lyla, "is that we don't see whoever killed Mamadou brought to justice."

"In light of what we know now, it seems pretty certain that he was murdered. But whoever was responsible has done a damn good job of covering his tracks. We can't go to the police without any proof so the best we can do is try to prevent it from happening again. And I will recommend to the underwriters that they require the mine to change security companies. Meanwhile, I'd like to be around when you stage your discovery to make sure it all works out. But it will mean delaying my departure for a couple of days. And it leaves the problem of what to do today," said Conner giving Lyla a wink.

"Oh, I'm sure you'll think of something," Lyla teased, gently kissing his neck. "But we might be late for breakfast."

They decided to take a trip to the company beach house for the day. The drive took them through the oil palm plantations which were replaced by coconut palm plantations as they got closer to the coast. They saw the locals making charcoal from the coconut shells. Piles of empty coconut shells were put in pits and set on fire. Then they covered the pits, limiting the oxygen, and let them smolder before extinguishing the fire completely. What was left was charcoal. When everything had cooled down, the charcoal was loaded into sacks and sent by truck to the city.

They followed a small dirt road which paralleled the beach until they finally arrived at the guest house. And they weren't disappointed. The house was small and rustic but had everything they needed. And the beach was idyllic. Miles and miles of fine white coral sand lined with blue ocean and palm trees. A housekeeper and caretaker couple lived on the property and were notified in advance of their visit. The housekeeper prepared a delicious lunch while Conner and Lyla walked on the beach and swam in the warm salty water of the Atlantic Ocean. After lunch they relaxed in hammocks in the shade. Time drifted by as they talked and enjoyed the warm ocean breeze and listened to the waves crashing on the beach. Late in the afternoon, storm clouds started gathering so they drove back to the Chateau.

Monday morning arrived and Conner and Lyla went about their routines as they normally would. Lyla went for her run and Conner met me in the garden feeding the goat. I remember there was a foggy haze that morning and I was surprised to see Conner emerging from it and walking towards me across the lawn.

He could see my surprise and grinned at me as he got closer.

"I thought you'd already left," I said.

"Having too much fun," replied Conner. "Decided to hang around a little longer."

Lyla and Conner drove to the mine and Conner spent some time working on his report in the engineering office so Lyla could be on her own to carry out her plan. She stuck to her normal routine by going to her office first and making coffee. After checking the weekend production reports, she put on her hard hat and started her walk about. She eventually made it to the ponds and stopped by the corner of the preg pond where she had seen the camouflaged figures. She noticed that two of the bird balls were sitting a little lower in the water than the others. She called the plant operator over.

"Akwasi, can you see those partially sunken balls?" she said pointing them out to the operator. "Please check them to make sure they don't have leaks."

Akwasi went and got a pole to fish them out. While he was attempting to extract them from the pond, he noticed the strings and then the ropes. He got an assistant to help him and they hauled the sacks up and opened them finding they contained carbon.

"Why are the sacks of carbon in the pond Miss Lyla? "Who would have put them there?"

Akwasi was good with machinery and working with his hands, but new to gold processing.

"It looks like someone is stealing gold Akwasi," answered Lyla. "The gold in solution will stick to the carbon, and who-ever put the sacks there was probably planning to return and take them away with a fair amount of gold."

Lyla asked Akwasi to check the rest of the pond for any more sacks and went to see Bamba. She explained to him what was going on.

"How can that be? There must be some mistake. Some reasonable explanation. My people wouldn't let something like that happen," protested Bamba.

But Lyla showed him the evidence and he promised a full investigation.

"Let's go and check the video monitors," suggested Bamba, knowing full well that that corner of the pond was not covered.

They checked the monitors and found that in fact there was no coverage in the spot where the sacks were discovered. But the areas around it were. Bamba said they would review the weekend tapes to see if they could see someone coming or going with unexplained sacks.

Lyla told Bamba she would have one of the plant operators check all the ponds each shift to prevent it from happening again.

Word of the gold theft travelled fast. I was practicing piano with Roland when Konaté barged in. "We need to talk. In Private," he added scowling at me.

I left the sitting room, closing the door behind me to go to the kitchen. When I reached the end of the hall, I heard the sitting room door open and turned my head around to see Konaté poking his big shiny head out of the doorway. It was obvious that he was checking to see that I wasn't listening at the door.

"Well they found it," said Konaté after he checked that no one was listening at the door. But it wasn't Conner. It was his little Australian whore."

"Found what?" asked Roland.

"The sacks of carbon in the preg pond. It was probably Conner's idea. You should have seen to it that he was on his way sooner. If he'd left after a week like initially planned, this wouldn't have happened."

"Oh Christ. Are they going to trace it to us?" asked Roland.

"Of course not. How could they possibly? That's not the problem."

"Then what is the problem?"

"The problem," said Konaté, "is that the General is not going to be happy when I tell him his gold supply has been shut down."

"You're just going to have to tell him it's over. The well is dry. He'll have to find some other source of income."

"Ha," laughed Konaté. "You don't know the General well after all. As long as this operation is producing gold he'll be taking a piece of it one way or another. I'll tell him we are working on a backup plan."

"And what would that be?"

"I don't know exactly, but I have some ideas," Konaté replied arrogantly. "I'll let you know in good time. But what I need you to do right now is to find out if the gold theft discovery is going to be a problem with Conner's due diligence. You're going to have to do some damage control. Convince him that the problem is solved and send him on his way."

Konaté left and Roland sat alone for a while wondering how it had gotten to a point that his operations manager was giving him orders. Then he went and found Jenny and asked her to invite Conner and Lyla and arrange a special dinner for tonight.

New Assignment

I knew something big was going on but had no idea what. Until I got to the kitchen. The news of the theft was already being passed around and embellished by the staff. At first I thought that was probably what Konaté had gone to tell Roland. But then I started to wonder. If what Konaté had to say was so terribly confidential that he needed to check at the door to make sure no one was listening, perhaps it was something else. After all, everyone at the mine and Chateau already knew of the theft. It had to be something more complicated than just reporting the theft. Was Roland involved somehow? And what about the conversation I'd overheard between Konaté and the General? I decided I should talk to Conner.

Conner and Lyla arrived back from the mine at around five o'clock. I met them coming in the front door and told Conner that I needed to talk to him privately. He said to meet him in the games room in half an hour.

I was waiting when Conner arrived. He and went to the fridge to get himself a bottle of beer. There was no one else around.

"How can I help you Kwame?" he asked.

"I overheard something I shouldn't have. I feel like I should tell someone, but I don't want to create any problems for anyone."

"Well I'm leaving tomorrow so I don't know if I can help you, but I'd be happy to hear what you have to say."

I felt that if anyone knew what to do, it would be Conner. So, I took a deep breath and told my story.

"I overheard Mr. Konaté and General Tiémoko talking. I only heard a bit. The General said "…plans to take him out so I can gain control of the government," " I said.

Suddenly, Conner looked grave and I wondered if I had made a mistake telling him.

He lowered his voice and said, "Would you please repeat that?"

I did, and he asked, "When did this conversation take place?"

"Friday night," I answered. "Actually, probably around one o'clock Saturday morning."

"Have you told anyone else?"

"Only my father. He said it wasn't my business and not to tell anyone else. And I wasn't going to. After all I might not have heard correctly. But then when I heard about the gold theft, I thought it might be related and figured I should tell you. I thought that because you are friends with Minister Djedje, perhaps you could get word to the President. You could warn him."

"You did the right thing Kwame. But don't tell anyone else. It might put you or them in danger. I'll make sure the President is warned. Minister Djedje is a close friend of his and would do anything to help him."

It was about an hour later that Roland poured Lyla and Conner drinks as they arrived in the upstairs dining room. I was serving the hors d'oeuvres when Roland held up his glass and said, "Here's to Lyla. Great work today uncovering this terrible gold stealing scheme."

The four of them enjoyed their drinks and discussed the events and mechanics of the theft while I lit the candles in the polished silver candelabras and filled the crystal water glasses on the dinner table.

"Do you think that the theft of loaded carbon could explain the discrepancy in the gold balance?" asked Roland.

"We went through the calculations this afternoon," answered Lyla, "and it seems entirely possible."

"Splendid," replied Roland. "So Conner, your report for the underwriter. It needn't have any caveats. It appears that we've eliminated the fly in the ointment," he added trying to draw Conner's conclusions and recommendations from him.

"Yes, a very timely discovery on Lyla's part," replied Conner neglecting to mention that he would be recommending a change in security providers anyway.

This news seemed to please Roland and he relaxed and became his usual self. The perfect host and orchestrator of a superb party.

After dinner Jenny talked a bit about her work at Nouvel Espoir and plans for the future. She produced photographs showing the evolution of the project. What the building looked like when they first bought it and how much better it was after being renovated. She also had photos of the staff and some of the new mothers and their babies.

"We're putting together an endowment to be used to continue the operation of the clinic after the mine is finished," she explained.

She asked Conner if he might approach his client, the financial institution that was investing in the operation, regarding a donation. Conner agreed and added that he had a few other ideas of organizations or individuals that might be interested in contributing. Lyla laughed and talked throughout the evening and didn't show her disappointment in Conner's pending departure.

After dinner, Conner and Lyla and made plans to meet in a couple of months. Perhaps in Paris. Conner didn't burden her with my news. With what I had overheard.

In the morning, they said their goodbyes and Lyla left for the mine while a driver took Conner to Abidjan.

Conner's flight wasn't scheduled to leave until the next day and he had made arrangements to meet with Leon Djedje at his office in the afternoon. After he checked into his hotel and dropped off his bag, Conner headed over to the Ministry of Energy and Mines.

After passing through several layers of security, Conner found Leon's secretary who brought him to his office. "Welcome back," said Leon rising from his desk to shake Conner's hand. "Come in and sit down my friend. Tell me, how was your visit?"

"I wish I could say it was straight forward, but it wasn't."

Conner summarized the week's events starting with Mamadou's drowning, the gold theft and finishing up with the bomb that I had dropped on him.

"Shit. I'll inform the President of what you just told me. He'll be able to add extra security. But we need to figure out a way to stop Tiémoko," said Djedje. "This is exactly what I was worried about. That guy is out of control."

"Can't the President just have Tiémoko arrested?" Conner asked.

"It would be difficult with hard evidence. Impossible without. Imprisoning your political opponents without proving just cause is frowned upon in most democratic societies. Tell me, what about your report to the underwriters? What are your conclusions?"

"I think I will end up saying everything is fine technically," said Conner. "But I think I need to recommend that the mine change security providers. And I know quite well how that will work out."

"That news will definitely not be received well by the General. And it will likely cause a lot of pain and anguish for everyone around him."

"Yes, and I'd prefer to be on the other side of the Atlantic when that happens."

"Listen Conner, there's something I need to do right now. Are you available for dinner tonight?"

"For sure. What time?"

"I'll pick you up at your hotel at seven o'clock."

Conner was waiting in the lobby when Leon arrived.

"I know a place just around the corner," said Leon and they set off. "It serves excellent African and European food."

The restaurant was crowded and noisy and Leon asked for a table off in the corner. When they were seated, ordered drinks.

"Well you're looking fit and tanned. Life at the Chateau must agree with you," commented Leon.

"I'll bet I've lost ten pounds since I arrived. I'm just not accustomed to the heat and the humidity."

"I forgot to ask you how thing went between you and the Plant Manager?" Leon queried.

"Quite well," grinned Conner. "We're actually planning to meet in Paris in August."

"That sounds vaguely like a "commitment"" said Leon. "You're not giving up your "no commitment" principles, are you?"

"You just wish you were in my shoes."

Leon laughed and changed the subject. "President Bakayoko is grateful to you for passing on the information."

"You talked to him this afternoon?"

"Yes, I met with him and the Chief Inspector of the Judicial Police. They are taking this seriously. They have been trying to find a reason to arrest Tiémoko but haven't been able to catch him doing anything that would justify it. But what you have found out about the General stealing gold from the mine is a breakthrough."

The drinks came and they both ordered their meals.

Leon raised his glass to the Spirits and spilled a little of his drink on the floor.

"The President and the Inspector are thinking that if they could catch Tiémoko stealing gold from the mine, that would be enough to bring him down," Leon continued.

"In that case, it's unfortunate that we put a stop to the hidden carbon scheme."

"It would be my guess that they will come up with a new one. His brother-in-law, Adjobi Konaté learned from the best gold thieves around when he worked in Ghana. Either way, he is bound to make some other slip up. But we need to be watching closely."

They finished their drinks and Conner motioned to the waiter to bring another round.

"That's where you come in," said Leon.

"Me?" said Conner doing a double take. "I do mining engineering, not covert rogue general surveillance."

"I understand that. But you could still keep your eyes and ears open. If you could anticipate a time and place we might catch Tiémoko carrying out an illegal act or with some type of incriminating evidence, we could have the Judicial Police Force waiting to arrest him. You were successful the last time. President Bakayoko would be grateful and said he would pay whatever you feel the assignment warrants."

"But I need to turn in my report to my client. Underwriters are not known for their patience."

"Is there a way around it?"

Conner thought a moment and said, "I guess I could send it in by fax or courier. The way I see it, it will shake out one of two ways. Either we catch the General in the act, arrest him for theft and send him to jail which would also solve the security problem, or, the Ivory Coast ends up the site of a bloody coup which will scare off the underwriters and stop the financing regardless of the security issues at the mine."

"So, we can count on you?"

"As a personal favor to you Leon, I will give it my best shot. But if things get dangerous I'm out of here. Remember, I'm into consulting, with a bit of women chasing and beer drinking on the side. Not risking my neck over a cause that doesn't concern me."

You Mean They Killed Him?

The next morning, I was cleaning windows in the main entrance to the Chateau just outside Roland's office when Leon called on the phone. "Listen Roland, I am calling for two reasons. "I have some good news and some not so good news."

"First, I wanted to let you know," Leon continued, "that your application for the Mineral Exploration Concession to the north of the mine has been processed and approved by our legal department and I will be signing the resolution in the next couple of days."

"That's terrific Leon. We are eager to get started doing definition drilling and outlining more gold reserves. Thanks for letting me know," answered Roland.

"The not so good news is that the Ministry of Industry has requested that we conduct a full inquest into the accidental death that occurred at the Abengourou Mine last week. That means a detailed investigation into the circumstances. In addition, we are going to need to carry out a complete audit of the safety procedures of the mine with the intent of preventing future accidents."

"Of course, how can I help?"

"As you are aware, we are proud to have your company working in our country. And we know that you are using the latest technology and the highest standards in mine safety. We are impressed by the safety procedures you have adopted from South Africa and North America but because of the accident, because a man drowned in a cyanide solution pond, a number of questions need to be answered."

"I think it sounds like a bit of a witch-hunt, but I appreciate your position Leon."

"We need to have a consultant spend some time, perhaps a couple of weeks at the operation."

"Definitely, that would be no problem whatsoever. Starting when?"

"Tomorrow if that's all right. You already know him. We have contracted Conner Jackson to do the job. He is in Abidjan now but will head back to Abengourou this afternoon."

There was a brief but notable silence on the phone while Roland collected his thoughts.

"Wonderful," he said. "Conner is already familiar with the people and the operation. Perfect choice."

"Of course, the Ministry will cover the cost of his room and board."

"Nonsense, we have plenty of room at the Chateau and it is our pleasure to help," replied Roland.

"I knew I could count on you my friend. I will let you know when the resolution is signed and the Concession Assignment Contract is ready."

Roland hung up and put his face in his hands with his elbows on his desk. "Shit!" he said out loud looking at his watch and deciding it was too early for a drink. Instead he went downstairs to Konaté's office and told him about the conversation.

"You should have told Djedje we were too busy to have someone hanging around auditing our safety procedures right now," barked Konaté. "Now we're stuck with that stupid meddling Canadian for another two weeks," he added as he wiped the perspiration from his shiny head.

"Perhaps, but it is of the utmost importance for us to get that concession," retorted Roland. "And it was made quite clear that his help and our help go together. Anyway, it's done, and we'll have to make the best of it. Besides, a fatal accident is something deserving of a full investigation."

Konaté leaned back in his chair, fiddled with his enormous gold rings and looked up at the ceiling for a moment. He got up and walked around his desk to close his office door and said, "I wasn't going to tell you this, but I probably should, before you mess something up. It wasn't a "fatal accident." Mamadou didn't slip and fall in the pond. He was out there at night when our men were changing the carbon sacks and he saw what they were doing. They had to get rid of him."

"You mean they killed him?"

"Yes Roland, that's what I mean."

"Christ almighty! There had to have been a better alternative. Why didn't you check with me? Why would they kill someone over a few ounces of gold?"

"Calm down Roland. There was no alternative. And no time for discussion. The security team is trained to deal with problems like this," assured Konaté. "And besides, it's more than a few ounces of gold. We're talking several thousand ounces a year."

"This is crazy. What if someone gets suspicious? And what if someone finds out you killed Mamadou?"

"They won't. But we still have to divert suspicion whenever possible. Like putting the blame on Lyla. You see now?"

Roland was quiet for a moment, letting the pieces fall into place. "Perhaps, but I don't like it one fucking bit. I never agreed to be part of a scheme that had people killed. I want it to stop right away."

"It's not that easy Roland. Like I already told you, Tiémoko has grown accustomed to having this income to finance his lofty goals. Trying to cut that off would be like trying to tell an addict that he can't have any more drugs. And we're dealing with a man addicted to power. He will stop at nothing to get what he wants. Saying "No" to the General is not an option."

"So, you're just going to develop a new method to steal goad from the mine while Conner is here investigating an accident which was really a murder?" said Roland sarcastically.

"Something like that. And Conner Jackson had better not get in my way for his own good."

Leon's driver brought Conner back to the Chateau late in the afternoon. I was quick and got his knapsack out of the back of the car and on my back before Conner had a chance to protest. We walked toward the front door and Jenny came out to greet Conner. I kept moving but could see Jenny throw her arms around Conner and give him a big hug and kiss.

"Welcome back Conner," said Jenny refusing to give up her grip on him.

"Thanks for putting up with me again."

"No trouble at all," she said wrapping herself around his arm and walking inside with her guest.

I had taken Conner's knapsack to his room and waited for him to arrive in case he needed anything. He motioned me back into the room and closed the door.

"Kwame, I passed on the information you gave me, and it was brought to the President's attention. He is terribly grateful."

I was happy to hear that I was able to help. It made me feel proud about what I had done. "What's going to happen now?" I asked.

"The President's security team will increase the security level. But I'd like you to watch and listen. We think the General is involved with the operation that was stealing gold from the mine. There may be plans to do it again. And if we can help the police catch him, they could put him in jail. Please let me know if you hear anything else suspicious."

"Sure Conner, I'll do my best."

"But listen Kwame. Whatever you do, be careful! If you get caught sticking your nose where it shouldn't be, you could lose your job or worse. So, don't do anything foolish."

I left Conner's room and walked down the stairs to the main floor and almost bumped into Konaté.

"Where have you been boy?"

"I brought Mr. Jackson's bag to his room."

He looked at me for a second as if to say, "Are you hiding something boy?" but then said, "Go and wash my car. It's covered in mud and looks disgraceful."

The Furnace

Conner was waiting for Lyla when she arrived back from the mine. Lyla had no idea that he had returned and was a little later than usual. It was raining, and she didn't notice him as she parked her pick-up and hurried through the downpour to the Chateau entrance. Conner stood there grinning as she realized he was there. Lyla smiled, put her hands on her hips and said, "Just like a damn boomerang. Keeps coming back."

After a warm hug, Lyla asked Conner what was going on. "Long story. How'd you like to hear it over dinner at the Resto?"

Lyla quickly got changed they headed out. The rain had stopped, and Lyla drove while Conner explained that "officially," he had been contracted to investigate the fatal accident and perform a safety audit.

"But the real reason Leon wants me here is to help find a way to catch the General stealing gold from the mine."

They arrived at the restaurant and sat down at one of the many empty tables. The owner remembered them and said, "Guinness. Right?"

When he brought the beer, they ordered their meals.

"Since when does the Ministry of Energy and Mines care about theft at mines? Shouldn't that be the concern of the mining company or the police?"

Conner gave Lyla the background on what I had overheard the General telling Konaté and explained that the real issue was the political struggle between the General and the President and the possibility of a military coup.

"How does Leon expect you to find a way to catch the General stealing gold?" she asked. "We just put an end to that scheme."

"That's a good question. But there are lots of ways to steal gold from a mine, and we'll just have to assume that Konaté will figure out one of them. Apparently, his experience in the mines in Ghana taught him a few tricks."

"I wouldn't know much about that," said Lyla.

"No? The Australians have the reputation of being the best gold thieves on the planet."

"That legend was probably made up by a Canadian trying to divert the attention from himself."

"You may have a point. But the bottom line is that we don't believe the General is going to give up that easily. So, we're going to have to figure out how they're doing it and how to prove the General's involvement. Leon said he would send in the Judicial Police to arrest him if we thought there was a time and place we could catch him with some gold or doing something incriminating."

"At least now we know we are looking for theft, not erroneous assays. It should help us focus our investigative efforts," said Lyla.

I continued doing my duties around the Chateau and listening to what I could but didn't come up with anything. Konaté seemed suspicious of me and sometimes I could see him watching me or checking on me. He and Roland had had several closed-door meetings over the next couple of days and Roland seemed to be under a lot of stress.

One afternoon, Nsia asked me to take a tray with tea up to Miss Jenny in her room.

"Please don't make me do that Nsia. I don't want to go into her room."

Nsia laughed and said, "Just tell her that you need to get back to the kitchen right away."

I didn't protest strongly because I knew Konaté and Roland were talking in Roland's sitting room and I thought I might overhear something as I passed by. If I was going to hear anything about gold theft or political uprisings, it wouldn't be in the kitchen. I needed reasons to move around the Chateau. Unfortunately, the door to the sitting room was closed but I could hear raised voices inside. Konaté and Roland were arguing about something, but I couldn't quite understand the words. I paused in front of the door to see if I could make out something but just then, Jenny's door opened, and I had to continue my journey.

Jenny, who appeared to be wearing only a robe, leaned against one side of the door and said, "You can put the tray on the table over there," pointing inside the room.

"I'm sorry Miss Jenny but I need to hurry back to the kitchen," I said and thrust the tray at her, turned and quickly left.

She must have had a good laugh at me running off like that.

That evening, Ronald told Jenny what he had learned about the circumstances surrounding Mamadou's death.

"What are you going to do?" asked Jenny.

"I don't know. The whole racket should be shut down but if I expose the General, he'll have me killed for sure. I had no idea they would go this far. The whole affair makes me sick to my stomach."

"I'm sure we'll figure something out Roland. And whatever it is, remember I'm with you all the way."

Conner and Lyla went about their business for the next couple of days, all the while checking various places potential theft could occur. Conner spent a fair amount of time in the Process Plant documenting the circumstances of the accident as well as visiting back and forth across the mine site documenting safety practices and listening and watching. On Friday morning he was in the plant and noticed the door to the Gold Room was open. Inside, a plant operator with his helper were performing maintenance on the furnace.

Conner nodded good morning and continued on his way. Shortly after, he went to Lyla's office and asked her if she knew about the work being done on the furnace.

"Yes," Lyla confirmed. The operator checks the furnace after each pour and if there are any damaged refractory bricks, they are repaired or replaced."

"And the guys doing the work, Are they trustworthy? You know them well?"

"Akwasi? Yes, I know him well. He has been here since the mine opened. Completely trustworthy. His helper is new. I don't know much about him."

"Good. Just to be sure, let's check out their work this afternoon."

They waited until after five o'clock when most dayshift people had left and made their way to the Gold Room. When they arrived at the door Conner said, "For the sake of the surveillance cameras, let's just make this look like a routine check. No matter what we find."

Lyla nodded while entering the combination in the lock and Conner pulled the heavy door open.

They walked around the room and Lyla pretended to be checking the slag storage and gold bar molds while Conner went over and checked the furnace. It was easy to see where one of the refractory bricks in the bottom of the furnace had been replaced. It looked new compared to the rest and had new refractory cement around it. He reached in and ran his finger along the cement filled space between the new and old bricks. Sure enough, his finger ran up against a small point barely protruding out of the cement. But definitely pointed and hard like steel. He stepped back from the furnace and pretended to continue his inspection of the asbestos suit and gloves used by the furnace operator.

Conner held up the asbestos hood and facemask to show Lyla and said quietly, "Run your finger along the fresh cement line in the furnace where a brick has been replaced."

Shortly after, she made her way over to the furnace, looked around a while and reached into the furnace. Showing no sign of noticing anything, Lyla stepped back from the furnace, finished her inspection and they left, locking the great door behind them.

Neither said anything until they were in the pick-up returning to the Chateau.

"I felt a sharp point," Lyla said. "Is that what you meant?"

"Yes, exactly. Do you know what it was?"

"No idea. It felt like the point of a nail or something."

"That would be my guess," said Conner. "It's an old trick. Instead if using a four-inch-thick refractory brick, they put in a two-inch piece of wood and a two-inch-thick brick on top, with a nail sticking up to the top of the cement. When the furnace gets hot enough, the nail melts and the wood vaporizes. The molten gold runs down the nail hole and fills the void left by the wood forming a nice gold bar which can be recovered next time the furnace is maintained."

"You know what I think?" asked Lyla. "I think the Canadians must be at least as crooked as the Ghanaians for you to know all that. Do they teach you that in "Gold Stealing 101?" "

"It seems the gold mining industry attracts all sorts of bad actors," Conner laughed. "And I come from a long line of miners. My uncle was a prospector. He would take filings from a gold wedding ring, put them in a shotgun shell and shoot it at a quartz vein on his claims. He'd show this to prospective buyers and their eyes would pop out of their heads. They would fall over themselves making offers."

"Crikey! You have larceny running in your veins?"

"Perhaps that's why I have a nose for it. So, despite being an honest person, Akwasi most certainly did it. Somehow, someone has gotten to him."

"Likely Konaté or the General's staff."

"Yes, and this is the break we've been waiting for," said Conner. We can't let them find out that we know what's going on."

Security Head Lokossou Bamba lived in a rented house in Abengourou with his wife and children. The family was just sitting down for dinner when the phone rang. It was the technician from the surveillance monitoring center calling.

"You asked me to let you know if anyone entered the Gold Room sir."

"Yes, go ahead."

"The Plant Manager and the Canadian engineer just spent about ten minutes there. They didn't leave anything or take anything. It just appeared to be a routine inspection," the voice said.

"Ok, fine. Are they still at the mine?"

"No, they just left."

"Alright. Let me know if they return over the weekend."

Turning Point

The next day was Saturday and Conner and Lyla returned to the mine late in the morning. Lyla asked Akwasi to come and see her in her office.

"Yes Miss Lyla?" said Akwasi when he arrived. "What is it?"

"Please sit down Akwasi. Would you like some coffee or water?"

Akwasi declined the drink but took a chair beside Conner.

"Listen Akwasi," said Lyla leaning forward in her chair. "I know you are a good man and would never get involved with stealing anything, but we know about the furnace and need to find out who is behind it."

"I don't know what you mean," he said looking over at Conner and realizing he had walked into a trap.

"Akwasi, I know you didn't do this on your own. You're not in trouble. But it is extremely important that you work with us so we can bring whoever is behind it to justice."

Akwasi's lips started to quiver. When he spoke, it was in a whisper, "He said they would kill our families if we didn't do what he said."

"Who? Who said that Akwasi?" asked Lyla.

Without turning his head, Akwasi's eye's shifted to look through the glass window towards the surveillance camera in the corner of the outer office. "I can't be seen talking to you like this."

"Can we meet somewhere? Somewhere safe?" asked Lyla.

"Abengourou Central Park at ten o'clock tomorrow morning. I will tell you then."

"Don't worry Akwasi. Everything will be ok," Lyla assured.

Akwasi left hurriedly and Lyla said to Conner, "It sounds like we were right."

"Yes, and by the way he looked at the security camera, it makes me pretty confident that "they" are the security force or someone in the department. Someone with access to the monitoring system. We'll know more tomorrow."

Bamba answered his home phone and listened to his security technician's report of Conner and Lyla's return to the mine and the brief meeting with Akwasi.

"Do you think he told them what was going on?"

"Probably not, the meeting was too short. Besides, it was obvious that Miss Townsend initiated the meeting and would have no reason to suspect the operator of doing anything wrong."

"Do me a favour," said Bamba. "Pay Akwasi a visit later on and tell him I said to remember how valuable his loved ones are."

On their way back from the mine Lyla and Conner stopped in my village. It was my day off and I was playing soccer with my friends. When I saw their pick-up stop, I hurried over to meet them.

"Have you returned to join us for another meal?" I asked. "I'll tell my mother."

"No, not today thanks Kwame," said Conner. "But I have a couple of questions for you if you have a moment."

"First, I wanted to check and see if you had heard or noticed anything going on around the Chateau like we talked about the other day?"

"No, nothing in particular," I answered. "Mr. Konaté has been careful about what he says when I'm around. The doors have been closed much more these days. Oh yes, and it seems that Mr. Konaté and Mr. Roland have had some kind of disagreement. I overheard them arguing but couldn't hear what they were saying."

"That's interesting. I wonder what they were arguing about. Let me know if you see or hear anything more. No matter how insignificant it might seem."

"Sure Conner. I'll pass on anything I hear. What was the second thing?" I asked.

"Do you need two more players for your game?" he said smiling.

"Of course," I answered. "But this time Miss Lyla must be on my team, so we have a chance of winning."

After the game, I walked them back to their truck.

"Conner, there is one thing I remembered, but I don't know if it will be of any help," I said. "Last Saturday morning, when I was in Abengourou, I saw the General's jeep parked in front of a commercial building, near the bus station. It didn't seem significant at the time but later I remember thinking that it was odd because I was told the General was in a hurry to return to Abidjan."

"Where exactly was his jeep parked?" asked Conner.

"Just down the street from the bus station. Across the street from the bank. The building had a sign out front that advertised "Currency Exchange."

"Thanks Kwame, we'll check it out," said Conner.

As they were leaving, I called, "Miss Lyla." She turned and looked back at me. "Thanks for putting us on the scoreboard."

The next morning, they parked Lyla's pick-up on the road beside the Abengourou Central Park and found a shaded bench to sit on. It was a few minutes before ten. They watched children playing and couples walking along the concrete pathways bordered by flowering shrubs. They waited for Akwasi until eleven and gave up.

"Something probably came up," they assured each other while silently both feared the worst.

Akwasi had disappeared from his house early Sunday morning. His body was found by one of his children Monday afternoon. Fifty meters into the jungle behind his house. Partly eaten by wild pigs. His wrists had been slashed and there was a bloody machete beside him. The official cause of death was determined to be loss of blood due to self-inflicted wounds.

The unofficial cause of death, and the one that was discussed in the kitchen, was that the Spirits had pushed him down, causing him to fall on his machete to revenge his participation in the extraction on the Spirits' gold. No one quite knew why they chose Akwasi, which resulted in endless speculation.

Lyla was devastated by the news. She didn't touch her dinner Monday night. While I cleared off the table she and Conner walked out onto the terrace.

"I feel like it's my fault that Akwasi killed himself," said Lyla. "I should never have confronted him."

"That's not true," said Conner, anger welling up inside him. "He was being extorted by whoever threatened to kill his family and probably figured suicide was the easiest way out. You can't be expected to ignore your employees' stealing from the mine because you don't want to upset them."

"I guess you're right. But I still feel badly about Akwasi and his family. I'm not cut out for this. I should just head back to Australia and get a nine-to-five job. At least no one would be losing their lives."

"We all feel badly. And one way or another, we're going to catch the people responsible and make sure they get what they deserve."

While they looked up at the stars in silence, Conner thought to himself, "I'm not leaving here until someone pays for these deaths."

The Plan

Tuesday morning, they returned to the mine. Conner kept up his guise of conducting a safety audit and Lyla went about her business in the plant. Both kept an eye on the Gold Room. They decided not to confront Akwasi's assistant for fear of making the thieves aware of their suspicions. They needed the gold theft to be successful if they were to catch the General.

As they passed through my village on their way home, Conner remembered the comment I had made Saturday about seeing the General's jeep in Abengourou. They decided to stop and check out the place. As I had told them, the sign said "Échange de Monnaie/Currency Exchange" but in smaller letters it said "Instant Loans, We Buy/Sell Gold & Silver. Meilleurs Taux en Ville/*Best Rates in Town.*"

Lyla waited in the truck while Conner climbed the stairs and entered the building. Inside was one large room with several windows for tellers. Only window had an attendant. He was a scruffy looking character with half burned cigarette hanging from his lips and a bored look on his face. Perhaps sixty years of age, olive skinned, he looked like the owner or family of the owner. He didn't say anything as Conner reached the window, just raised one brow as they made eye contact.

"I'd like to change some US dollars to CFA's (Central African Francs)," Conner said.

"How much?" he grunted with a strong Lebanese accent.

"A hundred," answered Conner.

The attendant put the cigarette down in the ashtray and scribbled a number on a piece of paper and slid it under the barred window.

Conner looked at the paper and said, "That's significantly lower than the published rate."

He picked up the cigarette, took another drag and exhaled. "Hey, four-thirty in the afternoon," he said pointing at a clock on the wall. A slight grin forming on his lips. "The banks are closed. Take it or leave it. Like our motto says, "*Meilleurs Taux en Ville.*"

Conner wasn't short of CFA's but handed over his hundred dollars to keep the interaction going. The attendant examined each bill carefully to make sure none was counterfeit as he counted them. Then he pulled out a bundle of CFA's as big as a coconut and started peeling off notes.

"You also buy gold here?" inquired Conner.

"The best prices around."

"In what form?"

"Any form as long as it has gold in it."

"What about panned concentrates?"

"Like I said, if it has gold in it, I'll buy it. Panned concentrates, mercury amalgam, jewelry, coins, furnace ash, plating waste, whatever," the attendant said butting his cigarette out in the overflowing ashtray. "You have some?" he asked, trying not to look too eager to conduct some business.

"I have a friend who might have some for sale," said Conner with a grin.

"Tell him I can pay top price," he said as Conner turned around and left.

He filled in Lyla on the way back to the Chateau.

"I bet the General is selling the stolen gold to this guy," said Conner.

"What about the carbon? I can't see him hauling sacks of loaded carbon into that little office."

"No, likely his personnel delivered it to a warehouse or some treatment facility where the gold was extracted and the General just goes in to pick up his cash. The question is, "will he bring a gold bar in?""

"What else would he do with it?" Layla remarked. "I don't think he'd want to take it back to the city and start dealing with a new buyer. That would just increase the chances of somebody getting suspicious."

"I agree. He already has an arrangement with this Lebanese guy who seems like the type to know when not to ask questions. And if the General sticks to his schedule, he will show up at the mine Friday afternoon and go to see the gold trader Saturday morning. That would be a perfect place to catch him."

Conner called Leon and filled him in. Leon asked Conner to come to Abidjan in the morning to map out a course of action together.

"Great work Conner," said Leon as Conner entered his office. After they shook hands, Leon asked, "How much gold do you think he will be carrying?"

"I can't say for sure, but my guess would be that the bar will be about five centimeters thick by ten centimeters wide by twenty centimeters long. The same size but half the thickness of a refractory brick. With a doré specific gravity of around sixteen we are looking at about sixteen kilos. That would be worth about one hundred and sixty thousand dollars" he added.

"That amount of gold will be hard for him to explain," said Leon. "The question is, without proof that the gold was stolen, "how long will we be able to hold him?""

"What do you mean?" asked Conner, taken by surprise.

"The President has been conferring with the Supreme Court and they say that with the evidence, meaning the gold, Tiémoko can be arrested but we will need someone to testify as an eye witness or possibly some other proof that the gold actually came from the mine to make charges stick. It is highly likely he will be out on bail in a couple of days if all we have is the gold bar."

"And where does that leave us?" asked Conner. "He's going to know he was set up and probably by whom. And he won't be happy about it."

"You're right, so we've got to nail him the first time. Is there any way of proving the gold came from the mine?"

"Well, as you know, gold is gold," said Conner. "There is no way to prove its source. If the doré was exceptional in some way, perhaps with a unique impurity, it would be possible to make a good case for its origin. But as far as I know the gold from the Abengourou Mine is free of impurities that might give it a distinctive signature."

"What if we gave it a signature?" asked Leon. "What if we added something? Like a rare earth or radioactive mineral?"

"Where could we get access to something like that?"

"We have all kinds of stuff in the Ministry's Mineral Museum," said Leon. "I know we have some monazite crystals. Monazite contains thorium which is radioactive. Not strong radioactivity but powerful enough to be detected."

"I guess we could put some crystals in with the old slag or the electro winning sludge and they would be added to the pour," said Conner thinking out loud. "I don't know how much radioactivity would stay with the gold bar or if it would all get slagged off, but we could give it a try."

'Do we have time to add it to this week's pour?" asked Leon.

"Lyla is planning to pour tomorrow, Thursday, to leave time for the gold to be recovered by the thieves on Friday. We have time but will have to hurry."

"So, if the General were arrested Saturday, and the Police could hold him for a couple of days before he could get out on bail, we'd have until Monday to demonstrate that the gold came from the Abengourou Mine. The Ministry has a room full of instruments left by the French Geological Research Bureau. There's probably an old Geiger Counter there that we could use to verify the radioactivity of the gold bar."

"Then let's get down to the Museum and dig out those crystals."

The mineral museum was on the first floor of the building and was empty except for a security guard seated by the entrance. Leon explained that most of the visitors were groups of school children on field trips. There was pressure from the Finance Ministry to close the museum to save money, but Leon was a strong advocate of exposing the school children to the natural sciences and had been successful so far. They located the mineral case with a monazite crystal on display, pulled the case away from the wall and checked the drawers underneath for duplicates. They found a drawer containing six more crystals, so Conner put them in his pocket.

Next, they went to the storage room which was full of disorganized equipment and old instruments used in mineral exploration. The French government geological research team, Bureau de recherches géologiques et minières (BRGM), had spent many years mapping the geology and identifying mineral deposits in the former French colony. When they left they donated their equipment to the Ministry of Energy and Mines but most of it was never used. Conner and Leon rummaged through the piles of electronic equipment and eventually came across a Geiger Counter. They turned it on but found it to be completely dead. Conner pushed the battery test button and not surprisingly, the needle didn't react. Upon opening the battery storage compartment, it was obvious why. They pulled out he large square battery and found it covered in white and green corrosion. They scraped enough off to see that the battery was rated at six volts.

"Where are we ever going to find a battery like that?" asked Leon. "I haven't seen anything like that for years."

"No worry," answered Conner. "We'll just make one. You go to the store and buy four, one-and-a-half volt "D" cells, just regular flashlight batteries, and I'll put together a holder to connect them in series with some parts from these other instruments. Four one-and-a-half volt batteries will produce the same power as one six-volt battery."

Conner pulled out his Swiss Army knife and proceeded to take the screws out of another instrument while Leon left to find the batteries. A few minutes after Leon's return, Conner had the Geiger Counter up and running.

Setting the Trap

Conner drove back to Abengourou with the monazite crystals arriving at the Chateau at dusk. He and Lyla went to Resto for dinner so they could talk. The owner had two bottles of Guinness open for them as they sat down at the table next to the river. Conner explained about the need to have some hard evidence to be able to make the charges against the General stick. They ordered their meals and he went on to explain the plan to add radioactive monazite to the pour.

They looked out over the river at the shimmering of the lights of the restaurant as they reflected off the slowly moving water. Occasionally, a fisherman would paddle by in his rustic canoe.

"Conner, I'm worried that if the General is arrested and later freed, he'll be out for blood and we would very likely be near the top of his revenge list," said Lyla.

"Then we'll just have to make sure that he doesn't get off. Not only for our sakes, but for Mamadou and Akwasi."

"But what if he does?" she repeated.

"I know what you're saying, and I've been thinking about that too. If shit hits the fan, we'd better be on the midnight flight for Paris. Never to return. Maybe take a sailing trip around the Caribbean."

"I guess that's not a bad Plan B," she agreed as the owner arrived with their meal of captain fish and another round of Guinness.

The next morning, Conner and Lyla waited until the Gold Room was opened for the pour and the furnace operator was preheating the furnace. There were several plastic bags of black sludge that had just been cleaned out of the electro-winning circuit in a row on the floor in front of the furnace. This material would be melted in the furnace and transformed into beautiful gold bars. Conner and Lyla entered the gold Room and explained to the operator that they would be watching the pour as part of the overall safety audit. The roar of the furnace made talking difficult. Being careful to keep himself blocking the view of the surveillance cameras, Conner walked over to the slag bucket and dropped in the monazite crystals.

Taking notes and photos, Conner watched as the operator put the plastic bags of sludge in the furnace followed by the bucket of slag left from last week's pour. He added more flux which was mostly silica sand. The furnace roared while they waited for the mixture to melt. When it was ready, the mixture was poured into a set of cascading molds and four complete bars were filled with doré and the fifth contained mostly slag. While the bars were still molten, the operator took samples by inserting a glass tube into the bars which when extracted contained a thin sample of the gold. The samples were saved for a "referee" should the mine's assays differ too greatly from those of the refiner.

When the bars cooled, they were cleaned with a wire brush, the name of the mine was stamped on with a tooling die, and finally they were weighed. The armored car company, which had been waiting, took the bars and left. The new slag was put in the bucket along with any material swept up in the work area and the great door was locked once again.

I was playing cards and listening to music in the kitchen during my coffee break when they got back to the Chateau. Conner found me and asked me to meet him by the pool.

"Listen Kwame, I really need your help," Conner said.

"Sure Conner, anything," I said.

"As I mentioned before, we are going to try to have the General arrested, but we need all the evidence we can get. When he is here tomorrow night, I need you to do your best to listen to anything you can. Specially about his plans for Saturday morning. And fill me in before you go to bed."

"I'll do my best Conner. Normally, people say a lot of things around me that they probably shouldn't. I guess they don't see me as a threat. But, like I told you, Mr. Konaté seems suspicious of me lately."

"If that's the case, don't worry. And whatever you do, don't take any chances. The last thing we need is for you to get caught."

"Don't worry Conner. I'll be careful."

"Come to my room when the General goes to bed. Let me know one way or the other, it doesn't matter what time it is. Even if you heard nothing."

"Okay Conner. Got it."

Akwasi's helper had taken over his duties so the next day, he went to check the furnace and perform the routine maintenance. Lyla and Conner gave him lots of distance but kept an eye on his movements. When he finished he walked across the yard to the office building carrying his tool box on his shoulder. Conner followed a couple of minutes later and arrived just in time to see Bamba's office door opening and the helper leaving.

Conner went into the mining department offices but could still see Bamba's office door down the hall. In a few minutes Konaté showed up and also went into the Security Chief's office. The door opened shortly after and he left with a heavy looking package wrapped in newspaper. Conner returned to the plant.

While he was crossing the yard, he could see Konaté's car leaving the parking lot.

Conner drove into Abengourou where he had arranged to meet the Judicial Police. He showed them where the gold trader's office was located, and they worked out a plan to arrest the General, if and when he approached the building. Presumably around nine o'clock the next morning. The police had also posted someone at a check-stop on the highway back to Abidjan in case the General didn't go to the gold trader's office.

Konaté and the General stayed up late drinking brandy in the Drawing Room. The door was closed so I couldn't hear anything unless I put my ear right against it. Which I didn't want to do for obvious reasons. However, I found that I could hear most of what they were saying from the bathroom next door. The sound seemed to carry through ceiling from one room to the next, so I used a broom handle to push up one of the ceiling tiles and slide it away. I could hear the words the spoke quite clearly. And what I heard shocked me.

Caught

Nice looking gold bar."

"It certainly is, and that greedy little Lebanese better pay a good price for gold like this or he will be sorry. Was it difficult to have it made?" asked the General.

"Not really," answered Konaté. "We leaned on a pair of workers. Told them their family's wellbeing were at stake. Everything was fine until that stupid Canadian and his Australian girlfriend started questioning one of the workers. He didn't tell them anything, but he got scared and the stupid fool killed himself. The other worker seems to be able to handle things on his own."

"Everything comes at a cost. His life was just one sacrificed for a better future for our country," said the General.

"I'm sure the gold trader will be happy to purchase a fine gold bar like this one. You should tell him there will be lots more coming in the future," remarked Konaté.

"There likely won't be," noted the General. After I form a new government, I plan to nationalize the mining industry. And I would like you Adjobi, to be the new Minister of Energy and Mines."

"It would be my honor. When do you expect to carry out your plan to take out the President?"

"That's one of the things I wanted to talk to you about," explained the General. "I have contracted a fellow, a mercenary from Sierra Leon, to do the job Tuesday. He has his orders, has been paid and needs no further instruction to carry out his assignment. Parliament convenes Monday morning in Abidjan and when they recess for the day on Tuesday, at around one o'clock, the President will be taken by car from the National Assembly to the Presidential Palace. As his car travels along the Boulevard de le Republique, a missile will be fired from the roof of the Hotel Tiama, destroying the car and incinerating its occupants."

I couldn't believe what I was hearing and wanted to run to Conner's room and tell him everything. But I didn't want to miss any details, so I continued to listen.

"I will have troops stationed near the National Assembly and the Palace as well as the train station, airport and port. When the President's car is destroyed, I will give the word that we are under attack by rebels and until the situation has been stabilized, I am declaring martial law and assuming the position of interim President for logistical reasons. I will force the Vice-President to sign an order handing his authority to me. We will temporarily halt all travel and close the banks. Anyone that contravenes my orders will be arrested."

"How can I help General?" asked Konaté.

"I would like you to come to the Palace Tuesday evening. I know I can trust you and I will need you to help deal with any problematic members of parliament. I anticipate some will be questioning my authority and we'll need to lean on them to keep them in line."

"That sounds like something right up my alley," replied Konaté. "Anyone stupid enough to resist will be sorry."

"I'll let the Palace guards know to expect you. You should travel to Abidjan over the weekend and stay somewhere near the Palace."

"It will be my pleasure." The brandy must have gotten to Konaté because he said, "Excuse me one moment General."

I heard footsteps and realized he must be on his way to use the bathroom, but by then I didn't have time to leave. I grabbed the broom handle and started trying to slide the ceiling tile back into place but couldn't quite catch the edge of it and get it to move. When I heard the Drawing Room door close and Konaté's footsteps in the hall, I decided to hide in the cubicle. I stood on the toilet seat, crouched over and pushed the door closed so he wouldn't see in. "Perhaps the brandy would make him less observant," I thought. I heard him come in and use the urinal and then wash his hands in the sink. Just as I thought he was leaving the cubical door flew open.

"What are you doing here?" he demanded.

"I was using this bathroom without permission and didn't want to get caught so I hid in here," I answered.

"Don't lie to me you little shit. Do you think I'm stupid? You were listening through the ceiling," he said angrily as he grabbed me by the front of my shirt and dragged me out of the cubicle pointing at the missing tile.

"No Mr. Konaté, I promise. I wasn't listening," I pleaded.

"You're lying," were the last words I heard before he threw me against the wall and the lights went out.

When I awoke it was pouring rain. My hands and feet were bound and I had a gag in my mouth. The General and Konaté were loading me into the back of Konaté's car. I started to struggle and kick the car with my feet making muffled calls for help when Konaté picked up something heavy and hit me on the head again. I returned to my world of darkness.

Jenny was awake in her room at the front of the house and heard the commotion. She looked outside her window and saw what was going on. She woke up Roland and told him what was happening. By the time he got to the window, Konaté's car was pulling out of the gate and turning on to the road heading away from town. The General had already gone inside and headed to his room. Roland pulled on his housecoat and shoes and grabbed the revolver from his bedside table. He ran down to his jeep, jumped in and drove as fast as he could in the direction Konaté's car had gone.

What's Done is Done

The rough road wound downhill toward the river and then lev-elled out. A few minutes had passed and Roland was begin-ning to worry that Konaté had turned off somewhere when he rounded a bend and through the blurred windshield he saw the brake lights of a car, at the top of the next hill, pulling to a stop beside the road. When he got close he could see it was Konaté's vehicle and he pulled up behind it and got out. The car was parked at the top of a steep precipice. Below was the rain swollen river. Konaté recognized Roland through his side mirror.

"What's going on?" asked Roland as Konaté stepped out of his car.

"Nothing that concerns you Roland. Go back to bed for your own sake."

"Do you have the boy in there?" demanded Roland pointing at the back of the car.

"Roland, there was a problem. I'm taking care of it. Now leave before you get in over your head. This is your last chance."

"I'm not leaving until you release the boy."

"I'm sorry you had to see this Roland. This stupid boy was listening to private conversations. He heard things that can go no further. There is no way to get around what has to be done."

While Konaté was talking, he opened the back of his car and pulled my unconscious body out and I fell onto the muddy road. He was dragging me over to the cliff by my bound arms when Roland pulled the gun out of his housecoat pocket.

"That's far enough Adjobi," said Roland pointing the revolver at him.

Konaté looked at him and laughed. "You won't shoot me. I'm your meal ticket. And besides. If this kid talks, we all end up in jail. You, me, the General. Everyone involved. It's not nice but it's necessary. Now come here and give me a hand.

Konaté continued dragging my limp body and was about to give me the final push over the edge when the shot rang out. Konaté staggered and straightened up turning towards Roland. Blood soaking through his shirt near his waist.

"You shot me! You stupid shit!"

Roland pulled the trigger three more times in quick succession putting three bullets into Konaté's chest. Konaté staggered back one step and tumbled down the bank into the raging river.

Roland checked my pulse then removed the gag and untied my hands and feet. He stuffed my soaking wet body into the back seat of his jeep and drove back in the direction he had come. Instead of stopping at the Chateau he drove straight to the emergency entrance at the hospital. He explained to the emergency staff that he found me beside the road. Apparently robbed and beaten. I was still unconscious when they admitted me to intensive care and Roland left for the Chateau.

When he arrived back at the Chateau, Jenny, Conner and Lyla rushed out into the parking lot to meet him.

"Where is Kwame? Is he okay?" asked Conner.

"He's in the hospital. Unconscious. With a nasty blow to the head," answered Roland. "They're going to do some tests, but his vital signs are good. The doctor thinks he'll come around soon."

"What about Konaté?" asked Lyla.

"I don't know where he is. I was trying to follow him when I found Kwame dumped beside the road. There was no sign of Konaté. He probably thought Kwame was dead."

"Well, when he shows up, I personally will break his shiny fucking skull," said Conner clenching his fists.

"What do we tell the General?" asked Jenny.

"We don't tell him anything," said Conner. "He'll be leaving in a few hours, so we just play along like nothing happened. Then we can sort things out. He and Konaté probably think Kwame's dead. And we want them to keep thinking that."

Roland was badly shaken, and Jenny took him back up to their room. He explained to her but no one else what actually happened beside the road.

"I feel terrible," said Roland pacing back and forth. "But it was either Konaté or Kwame. Only one was leaving alive. And I chose Kwame."

Jenny sat down on the edge of the bed and said, "I don't envy you being stuck in that situation. The question now is, What do we do? How do we deal with it?"

"I'm thinking we should keep it to ourselves." Roland walked over so the window and looked out into the night. After a moment he turned to Jenny and said, "What's done is done. And telling the police won't bring him back."

Conner and Lyla went to the hospital. When they arrived, the night receptionist told them that I was in intensive care, still unconscious. They were instructed to sit in a designated waiting room and a doctor would come and talk with them when there was some news.

The waiting room was sparsely furnished with not much more than some plastic stacking chairs and a couple of tables strewn with worn out magazines. Several other worried looking people sat waiting for news of their loved ones' condition. After a couple of hours, that seemed like an eternity, the doctor came in and called their names.

"Your young friend has experienced a severe blow to the back of his head and is lucky to be alive," explained the doctor. "A couple of inches lower and the blow would have broken his neck."

"Is he conscious?" asked Lyla.

"He actually started coming around a while ago but because of the severity of the trauma, we put him on a coma inducing drug. It will reduce the amount of oxygen required by his brain until the swelling starts to subside. We'll continue this treatment for at least the next twelve hours."

"Do you think he'll be okay doctor?" asked Conner.

"He's young and strong and I would think any permanent damage unlikely. It's difficult to say at this point but we'll have a better idea when he wakes up."

"Can we see him?" asked Lyla.

"Not when he's in intensive care. But we plan to move him to a ward in the morning."

They went back to the Chateau and tried to get some rest, but after tossing and turning for a while, realized that sleep was not an option. Conner went to the kitchen and made coffee and they spent the next couple of hours talking in the games room. When the sun started to rise, Conner drove to my village. He told my parents I had been hurt and brought them to the hospital.

When they arrived at the hospital, I had already been moved into a ward with nine other beds, all occupied. When my mother saw me unconscious, with my head bandaged and an intravenous tube in my arm, she started crying.

"Who would do such a thing?" she wept and clutched my hand. "Kwame never hurt anyone."

"We don't know," Conner lied. "He was found beside the road. Probably robbed while walking into Abengourou."

"I think it was the Spirits warning him to mind his own business," said my father. "I only hope they have spared him his life."

It was almost nine o'clock, so Conner excused himself to take in the action at the gold trader's office. He didn't want to interfere with the Judicial Police's job, so he parked halfway down the block where he still had a good view. About fifteen minutes later, the General's car did indeed show up and parked in front of the office. The General got out and started walking up the steps with a weighty leather satchel in hand. Two Judicial Officers converged on him and met him halfway up the stairs. Another Officer attended to the driver to make sure he didn't attempt to assist his superior.

"General Tiémoko," said one Officer, "you are under arrest for suspected theft of gold from the Abengourou Mine. We are enforcing a directive issued by the Supreme Court of the Ivory Coast. You're going to have to come with us." They cuffed his hands behind his back.

A small group of onlookers was starting to form at the bottom of the steps.

"You can't arrest me. I'm the Major General. The Chief-of-Staff of the armed forces. Besides, you have no evidence."

"What do you have in the bag General?" asked the Officer.

"None of your business," snapped the General.

"That's what I thought. Let's go," said the officer as they took his satchel and hustled him into a waiting car ignoring his protests and threats.

Once the General was safely inside the car, they opened the satchel and looked inside then looked at each other with reaffirming nods. As they were leaving, they drove back up the street towards the spot where Conner was parked. Having to slow down for a pedestrian, the General had the opportunity to recognize Conner's face. He gave Conner a look similar to the one from their first meeting only this one said, "I knew you were up to something. And you're going to be sorry you screwed with me."

Coma

Conner returned to the Chateau and was met by the Lyla, Roland and Jenny. They were all eager for an update and pleased to hear that my condition was stable. Conner and Lyla had purposely avoided telling Roland, or anyone else about the trap set for the General. They wanted to ensure there were no leaks prior to his arrest. Now it seemed appropriate to release the news.

"Listen, has anyone seen Michael this morning?" asked Conner.

"I saw him heading toward the dining room a while ago," said Lyla. "Don't know if he's still there."

"There's something I want to tell everyone, and it would be better if we were all present."

The group headed downstairs to the dining room and there was Michael working diligently on a tall stack of pancakes.

"Do you mind if we join you Michael?" asked Conner as he pulled out a chair and sat down.

"Be my guests" replied Michael protectively moving the plate of pancakes a little closer.

Once they were all seated Conner said, "The General has been arrested for stealing gold from the mine. The Judicial Police caught him taking a doré bar into a gold trader's office a half an hour ago."

Roland looked like he was going to expire. He didn't know quite what to say. So many questions were going through his head. Above all, he had to be careful not to incriminate himself. He exchanged glances with Jenny and finally managed to stammer out, "How did he manage to steal a doré bar?"

"He had someone rig the furnace so some of the gold was left behind and recovered later by maintenance staff," explained Conner. "It's not that difficult when your people are also in charge of security."

There was a pause and Michael held up a finger while he swallowed what was in his mouth.

"How did the police know he would be carrying a gold bar?" he asked.

Conner explained how he and Lyla had discovered the operation and watched for the gold to go from the operator's helper or Bamba to Konaté and figured it would end up with the General.

"That reminds me," said Michael. "Konaté's wife called here this morning looking for him. She said he didn't come home last night."

Conner filled Michael in on the events of the previous evening. Michael was outraged when he found out that I had been beaten.

"Wherever he is he'd better pray I don't find him or I'll wring his bloody neck!" said Michael.

"What do we do about Bamba?" asked Lyla. "He played a key part in the theft."

"He did indeed, but he was only following orders from the General. We should wait and see what happens to the General before we try to nail Bamba," answered Conner. "What do you think Roland?"

"Um, yes," mumbled Roland looking quite unwell.

Conner answered everyone's questions as well as he could. When they were finished, Conner called Leon. He told Leon that the General was in custody.

"Wonderful news Conner. We are grateful for all you have done," said Leon. "The Chief Inspector told me he will need you to come to Abidjan to make a statement and show them how we can prove that the gold came from the mine."

"I don't think I'll be able to make it there tonight," said Conner thinking about Kwame and wanting to talk with him. "I'll plan on heading up tomorrow morning."

"Okay, and you should probably bring Lyla so she can make a statement as well. The more witnesses we have, the stronger our case will be."

"Do you have the Geiger counter?" asked Conner.

"You bet. See you tomorrow."

Conner and Lyla returned to the hospital around three o'clock. My father had gone home but my mother and her sister were back in the waiting room because the doctor didn't want me to be disturbed. Though I remained unconscious, the doctor had stopped introducing the coma drug to my intravenous supply. It was expected that I would regain consciousness in two or three hours.

Conner and Lyla sat and chatted with the ladies. My mother told them stories about me and my siblings. She told them the meaning of all her children's names. Kwame meant "born on Saturday". But, in fact, I wasn't born on a Saturday. Following tradition, the first-born son is named after his paternal grandfather, and my grandfather was born on a Saturday. She talked about each of her children even the two "gone but not forgotten" and it seemed to keep her mind off worrying about me. She said each of her children were given a special gift by the Spirits. Mine was my musical ability.

Shortly before five, the doctor opened the waiting room door and announced that I was "coming around and that everyone could return to my room for a brief visit."

I had been moved from the crowded ward to a private room for which, as instructed by Roland, Golden Sunshine was footing the bill.

Everyone rushed to my bedside and watched as I opened my eyes. My mother cried and told me that she was afraid that the Spirits were going to take me away like they did with the other two. She squeezed my hand as the other three stood back and watched.

Once she had composed herself I was sufficiently awake, the doctor intervened and checked me over. He shone a light in my eyes to check my pupils and made me follow his finger with my eyes as he moved it back and forth. He explained that I had been in an accident and was in the hospital and asked me a series of questions. "What is your name? How old are you? How many fingers am I holding up? Do you know what day it is? Do you remember the accident? What's the last thing you remember?

Unfortunately, things were foggy at best and although I answered most of the questions correctly, I could only remember events up until about midday Friday. After that it was a total blank.

My mother, however, was ecstatic that I seemed to be okay. She wasn't nearly as concerned about the events of Friday night as were Conner and Lyla. But they didn't push. After a short while, the doctor said he was pleased with my condition, but I needed to rest until tomorrow morning. They were all ushered out of my room and Conner and Lyla drove the ladies to my aunt's house in Abengourou.

I could remember that the General was planning to kill the President and that I was to try and overhear what I could. But I couldn't remember what went on. I had a fitful sleep. The nurses checked on me every hour. I had a splitting headache and dreamed that the Spirits were chasing me and throwing rocks at my head. I tossed and turned. I would awaken and realize I was in the hospital and wished it was all a bad dream. I was starting to think it just might be when the morning light began creeping into my room and the nurse bustled in and flung the curtains open. Then it all started coming back to me.

The Middle of Nowhere

The local police found Konaté's car Sunday morning. It was registered in the name of the mining company, so they brought it back to the Chateau. The rain had washed away any traces of blood and no one had an explanation as to why it was there or where Konaté might be. But the longer he was missing, the more the police thought he might have done himself in in connection with the General being arrested. Or made it look like he had killed himself and gone back to Ghana to avoid the same charges the General was facing. The local explanation, the one passed around the kitchen, was that he had stopped his car at the top of the hill to relieve himself and the Spirits pushed him off the cliff into the river. They believed that either the Spirits were unhappy because Konaté, as Operations Manager, was responsible for their gold being exploited or just because he was such a mean spirited arrogant person. Either way, not many tears were shed.

When I heard this later, I wondered if perhaps my wish had come true. That the Spirits heard me and had done away with him. Perhaps his death was my fault.

Conner came to visit me in the hospital early and found me eating breakfast and happy to talk with him. Because we were alone, he was able to tell me what he knew about Friday night's events. He said that Roland had followed Konaté and found me unconscious beside the road. That helped me put the rest of the pieces together and soon I had a pretty clear picture.

"It's going to happen Tuesday Conner. In Abidjan," I said closing my eyes tightly as the words I had heard came drifting back into my memory.

"What is going to happen?" asked Conner gently nudging but trying not to put too much pressure on me.

"I heard the General say that he had hired someone to fire a missile at the President's car from the roof of the Hotel Tiama as the President makes his way from the National Assembly to the Presidential Palace."

"Kwame, I'm so sorry about what happened to you," said Conner. "But what you have done for your President and your Country is monumental. I know President Bakayoko will be tremendously grateful. You may very well have saved his life."

I feeling of pride swept through me. I asked who else knew what went on that night.

Conner explained that as far as the hospital or my parents knew, I had been robbed while walking into Abengourou and it was best to leave it that way.

Just then my mother and father walked in. My mother was so happy to see me awake and eating breakfast that she started crying again. The doctor came in and explained that he was happy with my progress and optimistic about my recovery but would like to keep me in the hospital under observation for a couple more days.

Conner said that he had to go to Abidjan, wished me a speedy recovery and left. He wanted to hurry back to the Chateau to get word to Leon about the assassination plot as quickly as possible. He was driving Lyla's truck and almost at the Chateau when he noticed a vehicle parked on the side of the road up ahead. As he approached, the uniformed driver got out blocking the road and waving for Conner to pull over. Conner recognized him as Lokossou Bamba and pulled in behind the other car.

Being early Sunday morning there were hardly any people around and almost no traffic.

"General Tiémoko would like to talk with you," he said motioning toward the car.

"Last I heard, he was in jail," replied Conner.

"Not anymore. Please come with me," said Bamba.

Conner could see the General inside the car.

"Please join me for a short chat Mr. Jackson," said the General opening the door and leaning out.

"Sorry General. I've got things to do," Conner answered abruptly.

"Then you are under Military Arrest," said Bamba pulling his gun and pointing it at Conner, "for interfering with the General's ability to carry out his duties as Chief-of-Staff of the Armed Forces. Please get out and put your hands on the car."

"Or what? Are you going to shoot me?"

"Only if you refuse to do as you're told."

Conner thought about what happened to Mamadou and was quite aware that Bamba would probably relish any excuse to kill him, so he got out and turned slowly to reach for the roof of the pickup when the butt of Bamba's pistol struck him in the back of the skull. His legs buckled, and his body went limp. Bamba dragged him to the car and shoved him in beside the General.

When he awoke, Conner was lying on a concrete floor with his feet bound together and hands tied behind his back. Someone had just poured a bottle of water on his face. Sputtering, he blinked several times focusing his eyes. His head was pounding, and he felt like he was going to vomit.

"Glad to see you decided to come back and join us Mr. Jackson," said the voice belonging to the General but coming from the direction of two blurry dark objects.

Conner blinked some more and tried shaking his head, but it hurt too much. Finally, his focus sharpened enough to make out the General and Bamba.

"What's going on?" asked Conner.

"I'll tell you what's going on," said the General spitting on the floor. "I just spent the night in jail because of you. I'm a busy man with an important job to do. How do you think I like being locked up like an animal?"

"I'll give you a tip General. If you don't like jail, don't steal stuff."

The General walked over and kicked Conner in the ribs. "And a tip for you Conner. If you don't like my foot in your ribs, don't get smart with me."

Conner writhed on the floor trying to get his wind back while the General paced back and forth.

"I'm simply trying to figure you out Conner so please have the courtesy to be polite. What inspires you to come to my country and interfere in our affairs? What goes on here is not your business. You were hired to do an engineering study. When you are done you will return to your happy home and our business arrangements are not going to affect your life whatsoever. But still you feel the need to meddle."

"I don't like seeing innocent people hurt so a few greedy animals can help themselves at the trough."

"You just don't get it Conner. I don't do what I do to get rich. I have the material possessions I require. I don't crave cars and houses. I can't go into details, but my goals are far more significant. Vital to the nation. So be it if there are a few casualties along the way. I brought you here to explain this and show you what it's like to be locked up. Perhaps you will think about that next time you feel you must right every wrong you perceive in someone else's country."

"I'm sorry General, but you're delusional. Do you think you're God that you can throw people's lives away? You'd better find a new witch doctor because you need some serious help."

"Conner, my intension is to let you spend a few days here thinking about the ramifications of interfering in my business.

If, after that time, you can understand where you are not needed or wanted, I'll have you taken to the airport and put on a flight out of the country. But you are not making it easy for me."

"The easiest thing would be for you and your bug eyed sidekick to just go and fuck yourselves."

Bamba's leather boot struck him in the back carrying such a force that it sent Conner rolling over and left him gasping for air again.

"I think he needs some time alone to think things through," said the General.

"I think he needs a bullet in the head," replied Bamba as they turned out the light and left the building locking the steel door behind them.

Conner could still hear their voices on the other side of the door.

"Not yet. Perhaps he could be useful to us. Maybe his employer would be prepared to pay a ransom for his safe return? Give him some water and a bit of rice tomorrow. I'd prefer to keep him alive for now."

He heard the sedan doors close and the car's tires crunching on the gravel as it drove away.

Conner lay in the dark waiting for the pain in his upper back to subside while he pondered his predicament. He had himself to think about but also the President. After all, he was the only one I had told about the plan to assassinate the President. And I was unaware that he had been abducted.

Conner considered how this might play out. Since it was already Sunday and the General had indicated that he would like Conner to spend a "few days here" it was extremely unlikely that he would be released prior to the assassination scheduled for Tuesday. That was definitely bad news for the President.

"So, if and when I'm released," thought Conner, "it's likely that the General will be running the country. He won't be concerned any more with theft charges because he'll simply shoot or jail anyone who challenges him. The best possible outcome for me would be if he did what he alluded to and took me to the airport after three days and put me on a plane. But that's probably the least likely scenario."

The intense pain from the kicking was diminishing but Conner was still extremely uncomfortable. Lying on a concrete floor with his arms behind his back made it terribly difficult to find a position that didn't put a lot of direct pressure on some part of his body. He found that lying on his back, with his hands underneath him was the least agonizing but his arms and hands would go numb quickly. While he experimented with various positions he continued examining scenarios.

"The ransom scenario might be a possibility," he thought. "The brokerage house that's underwriting the project must have insurance. Probably with a kidnap and ransom rider. And although they don't really care about me, they wouldn't want to be seen leaving their contractors to die at the hands of despots. Though technically, I wasn't even working for them at the time of the kidnapping. But, even if the insurance company would cover it, the whole process could take months and there was a good chance I would die of some ailment or get killed for pissing off the wrong guy before I made it back to Canada. This scenario is a bit likelier but still a long shot."

The building made cracking noises as heat from the midday sun caused the steel roof and walls to expand. The temperature inside rose, and Conner started to sweat. He remembered the Swiss Army knife in his pocket, but it was useless to him because there was no way he could get his hand in the pocket of his jeans.

He had no idea what time Bamba would return tomorrow with water and rice, if at all. But if it was to be a full day later, he still had twenty-three or more hours left lying on the floor. All his moving and struggling had caused the ropes to cut into his wrists and ankles. As the temperature rose, the sweat caused the ropes to cut even deeper. There was a bit of light coming in through cracks between the ceiling and the walls so he could at least see. Four steel walls, steel roof, concrete floor and a door locked from the outside. Probably some kind of mothballed military warehouse or storage shed. At the far end of the building, Conner could see a large furnace or incinerator.

"The most likely scenario," imagined Conner, "is that they keep me here for a while. A few days or a week and get sick of taking care of me and the take me into the jungle and kill me. Or Bamba gets called away or arrested or killed and I'm left to starve or die of thirst. They wouldn't have left me somewhere that people could hear me call for help. I must be in the middle of nowhere."

He rolled over to the wall, lay on his back, lifted his legs in the air and kicked the corrugated steel cladding as hard as he could. Conner succeeded in making a momentous racket. He yelled for help and continued kicking for about ten minutes but all it got him was sore feet, a dry throat and the skin scraped off his hands which were rubbing on the floor the whole time. No one came.

"Yes, I am in the middle of nowhere," Conner decided. "And I'm fucked. And the President's fucked. And if I don't find a way to get the hell out of here, a few days from now, the President and I will both be strumming our harps on the "other side"."

Tired, Hungry, Thirsty and Sore

When Conner didn't come back from the hospital as expected, Lyla started to become concerned. She got Roland to drive her into Abengourou and spotted her pick-up parked down the road. She and Roland went in to check on me and I was still with my family. I told Lyla that Conner had left a couple of hours ago. Lyla used her spare set of keys to drive the truck back to the Chateau.

When they returned, there was a message marked "URGENT" for Conner to call Leon. Lyla returned the call instead.

"Hello Leon, this is Lyla Townsend. "I found a message for Conner to call you but I'm calling you because Conner is missing."

"That's certainly not what I wanted to hear. I was calling to let Conner know that the General was released from police custody early this morning."

"Oh shit. Do you think the General has something to do with Conner's disappearance?" asked Lyla.

"I guess that depends on whether or not the General was aware of Conner's involvement in putting a case together against him."

"I think he had a pretty good idea that Conner was behind it. Who knows? But I'm worried sick about what's happened to Conner."

"Don't jump to conclusions. Conner can take care of himself," said Leon trying to calm Lyla down. "I'll talk to the Judicial Police and see if there's something they can do. In the meantime, please let me know if you hear from him."

Lyla got in her truck and drove back into town. She drove up and down the main streets looking for any signs of Conner. She returned to the hospital, went to the admitting department and Rosie was on the desk again with a long line of people waiting their turn to talk to her. Lyla marched up to the front of the line and interrupting said, "Excuse me, but I have a question.

Recognizing Lyla, Rosie said, "Ma'am, could you please..."

"No" said Lyla slapping her hand on Rosie's desk so hard that her coffee mug bounced. "Could *you* please. My friend is missing, and I need to know if he was admitted to the hospital today. His name is Conner Jackson."

Looking indignant, Rosie checked a long list on a clipboard and confirmed that no one by that name nor any unknown patients had been admitted that day.

She tried to visit me again but visiting hours were over, so she returned to the Chateau.

Roland called the local police and asked if there had been any reports involving a person by the name of Conner Jackson. They promised to keep a look out for him but couldn't do much at this point.

Roland and Jenny did their best to console Lyla and assure her that everything would work out. But deep down, they all feared the worst.

Early that evening, Roland received a fax from the General.

"Roland, I'm being investigated by the Judicial Police for possible involvement in a gold theft ring from the Abengourou Mine. I was arrested with a gold bar in my possession. There will be a

hearing Tuesday in Abidjan and I need you to be there to explain to the court that the gold was payment for security services rendered. My lawyers will contact you. See you Tuesday."

Conner rolled and squirmed his way to the wall managed to sit himself up with his back against the steel siding. He looked around to see if there was something he could use to cut the ropes that were binding his wrists. The building was completely empty except for the furnace but he tried to identify something he could rub the ropes on. The heat was suffocating, and he was soaked with sweat.

"If I could only stand up," he thought. "I might just be able to reach something to cut these ropes. There's no way I going to escape if I'm tied up."

Conner bent his knees and pulled his feet up under him as far as possible. Then he leaned forward shifting his weight directly above the balls of his feet and was starting to stand up. He made it about half-way when he lost his balance and toppled over smacking his shoulder on the concrete floor.

"That wasn't such a smart idea," he thought as he lay on the floor. "But neither is laying here doing nothing." So, he tried again. On his fourth attempt, he stood up slowly arching his back and sliding his shoulders up the wall. He was pleased to find that there was enough slack in the rope around his ankles that he could shuffle his feet forward and backward about an inch.

He slowly made his way along the wall and checked for any flaws in the steel or imperfections in the welds. Perhaps the point of a screw or anything sharp enough the tear the fibers of the ropes. The movement of his feet caused the ropes on his ankles to burn his skin through his jeans. He made it to the first corner but found nothing. He was inching along the second wall when he noticed it was getting darker. By the time he got to the corner, the rain had started pounding down and the temperature started dropping to a bearable level. Moving along the third wall, he reached the door and light switch. He bent down and used his chin to turn on the light which consisted of an industrial fixture and bulb with a metal reflector shade above it.

"And then there was light," Conner said out loud. "Things are looking up," he thought. "Now let's have a look at the hinges on this door. It opens inward, so the hinge pins are on the inside. If I could slide the pins out, I could take it off the hinges and open it inward. Except my hands are tied. Shit."

Conner thought about the knife in his pocket and how he might be able to retrieve it. With his hands behind his back he was able to push the back of his jeans down. Using the door knob, he moved around pushing the sides and front down. They were already a bit loose because he'd lost some weight and before long he had them down past his hips. He wiggled and hopped and soon they were lying loosely around his ankles. He sat down, sliding his back down the door with his feet almost directly below him. He could clutch the loose jeans in his hands.

He methodically pulled at the jeans until his fingers felt the top of the pocket. He managed to get his fingers in and grabbed on to the knife. He pulled it out and stood up again. He opened the blade and held the knife in such a way that the blade was touching the rope, but he didn't have enough free movement in his hands to cut the rope with the blade. Pushing back against the wall forced pressure on the blade and likewise on the rope. So, he repeated the pushing back and bending his knees up and down. The strands of the rope started separating one by one. When the last one snapped, the rope came apart.

"I might just live. The President might live. We've got a whole new ballgame!"

Conner untied the ropes that bound his ankles and breathed a sigh of relief as he walked around the brightly lit shed stretching his sore muscles and joints. He was tired and hungry but the adrenalin in his veins pushed him on. He examined the hinges and tried to pry the pins out of the hinges with the screwdriver feature on his pocket knife, but they were in too tight. It would take a hammer and a four-inch nail to pound those pins out and he had neither.

It was dark outside by the time he sat back down and considered the pros and cons of his situation. "Pro: I'm free from the ropes. I have a chance to overpower Bamba when he returns. If he returns. Con: He has a gun and I don't. Pro: I have the element of surprise. As long as he returns before I pass out from fatigue or thirst or starvation. Con: He might not come alone. It wouldn't do me any good overpowering him if he has backup. Or he might not come at all. I'm going to need a good plan and a lot of luck."

Conner sat and thought about what he had for resources. He had his knife, his clothes. A few coins in his pocket. His wallet. He was thinking about how convenient it was that this apparently unused shed still had electrical service when it came to him. The electricity was the resource he needed.

He checked out the door and found that it was hinged to a wooden door frame so insulated from the rest of the building. The main power cable came from the outside, through the wall to a junction box. From there one set of cables went to the light switch by the door, another to the light fixture hanging from the ceiling and another to a plug socket on the adjacent wall. Conner used the screwdriver on his knife to open the plug socket and carefully disconnect the two wires, one white and one black. He checked which the live wire was by touching it to the steel of the shed. The shed was grounded so the live wire, the white one, gave a spark. He disconnected the black wire at the junction box and pulled backwards through its supports. He bared about a foot of it at one end and wrapped it around the hinge of the steel door. He went to connect the other end to the "on" side terminal of the light switch, but when the wire touched the terminal, sparks started flying. "Shit, the door must also be grounded," he thought.

Then he remembered that it was locked from the outside and the padlock latch was probably forming a connection between the door and the building. It needed to act as a live terminal, not grounded, to do its job.

"I'm going to need to turn off the light switch to connect the cable and keep it that way until the door is unlocked and no longer in contact with the shed. But I'll be working in the dark. I won't be able to see what I'm doing. The only other alternative is to wait until dawn to finish the wiring and I don't want to take a chance waiting until dawn in case Bamba returns sooner."

So, he disconnected the cable from the hinge and finished connecting the other end to the light switch being careful not to let the bared end come in contact with the shed. Then he turned off the light and by feel in the pitch black, wound the bared end around the hinge again.

Conner was tired, hungry, thirsty and sore but his spirits were lifted knowing he had an escape plan in place. He sat down and nodded off.

He had a fitful sleep, waking every fifteen or twenty minutes and checking to see if the morning light was coming in. Dawn finally arrived, and Conner could see his surroundings once again. He checked his handy work, and all seemed secure.

But no Bamba. Six o'clock, seven, eight. "Was he going to come?"

Conner's mouth was dry and his lips were starting to crack. He was worried, but he needed to keep his wits about him. He needed to remain positive and psyched up for what was to come next. At around nine-thirty, he heard a car approaching. He removed his tennis shoes and put them on his hands like a pair of gloves. He heard a car door slam and could see Bamba approaching through a narrow crack. The lock opened as did the latch, then the door opened enough for a hand to reach in and turn the light on just as Conner had hoped.

At that instant, Conner put all his weight into the door, slamming it on the arm. The current went through the door, into Bamba's arm and out the bottom of his leather boots into the wet ground. The overhead light dimmed and flashed while Bamba screamed. He tried to pull his arm back, but his muscles were paralyzed from the electricity pumping through them.

Conner thought about backing off but knew that if Bamba was still in good enough shape to get even, he would. So, he kept all his weight on the door until the screaming subsided and he could smell burning flesh. He turned off the light switch and opened the door. Bamba lay on the ground with his big eyes rolled back in his head and his feet twitching.

Conner put his shoes back on, stepped over Bamba and went to his pick-up to see if the keys were inside. They were still in the ignition and there was a bottle of water in the cup holder. He grabbed the bottle, put it to his parched lips and drank it eagerly. He was rummaging through Bamba's belongings to see if there was more when a shot rang out. He spun around to see Bamba's extended arm with his revolver in hand pointing at Conner fall to the ground and Bamba slump forward. A hole in the side of his skull oozed blood. At the corner of the building stood Michael Vandoorn with a hunting rifle up to his shoulder, and his big set of pearly whites glinting in the sunlight.

"Well I'm glad you happened to be in the neighborhood Michael," said Conner. "Nice shot."

"If you're going to survive in Jo'burg as long as I have, it's a mandatory skill."

Back to Abidjan

I suspected Bamba might have had something to do with your disappearance," said Michael handing Conner another water bottle. "So, when I saw him leaving the mine this morning, I followed him. I parked on the main road and walked up a path through the jungle so Bamba wouldn't see me. When I came around the corner he was aiming his pistol at you. So, I shot him."

"Well you saved my ass Michael. I owe you big time."

"What in god's green earth went on here anyway?" Michael asked looking at Bamba's scorched arm.

Conner recounted being brought by the General and Bamba and left with his hands and feet bound.

"I managed to get free of the ropes and put this together," he said as he showed Michael his improvised electric circuitry.

"What a stroke of genius, "said Michael. "Bamba must have been "shocked" to find out what you had been up to in his absence," he added chuckling and his own play on words.

Conner ripped the live cable out of the light switch so no one else would get hurt. They examined the furnace in the daylight and speculated that the loaded carbon had been "ashed" in it or burned until nothing was left but ash containing gold and that was what was sold to the gold trader.

As they left, Conner picked up Bamba's pistol and addressing his corpse said, "I think I'll be able to put this to better use than you." Taking Bamba's truck, he drove back to the Chateau with Michael following.

As Conner pulled into the parking area, the front door of the Chateau flew open and Lyla ran out to meet him. She was so happy she burst into tears. When she saw Conner's hands and arms, she ran to retrieve the first aid kit to treat the cuts on his wrists. Jenny asked the kitchen staff to prepare some breakfast while Conner and Michael recounted the events of the past twenty-four hours. Roland advised against telling the local police that there was a dead body that needed retrieving.

"The Judicial Police would be better suited to handle this," said Roland. "Otherwise you could end up with days of paperwork, or locked up, and turned over to the Military Police."

After he had eaten and cleaned up, Conner called Leon.

"Where are you?" asked Leon. "What happened to you?"

"Still in Abengourou," replied Conner. "I was kidnapped by the General and his Head of Security for the mine. I managed to escape but the security guy is laying in front of a warehouse in the jungle with his brains scattered all over the ground."

"I'm sorry Conner. We tried to keep the General in jail, but his lawyers managed to have him released. I called as soon as I found out he was free. Are you okay? What happened?"

"I'll fill you in on the details but first there is something more urgent to deal with. That plan to assassinate the President, it's scheduled for tomorrow."

"Oh my god. Are you sure?"

"Yes, the houseboy, Kwame, overheard Tiémoko and Konaté talking. They plan to do it as he drives from the National Assembly to the Presidential Palace. The poor boy was beaten and left for dead."

"That's terrible. I'll get word to the President right away."

"Good, but just to let you know, having the General in jail won't help anyway. He's hired someone else to do the job."

Conner briefly explained what transpired at the warehouse and Leon said he'd talk to the Judicial Police and find out how to deal with the situation. When Leon called back he told Conner that the Judicial Police were sending a team to recover the body and asked him to arrange for Michael Vandoorn to show them where to find it.

"There is a preliminary hearing into the General's involvement in the gold theft scheduled for nine o'clock tomorrow morning," said Leon. "The Chief Inspector needs you, Lyla and Roland to come to the headquarters today to make statements and meet with the Prosecutor. You and Lyla will act as witnesses and Roland, as Legal Representative of the Golden Sunshine Mining will need to formally file charges of theft on behalf of the Corporation."

"How is the boy?" Leon asked.

"Much better," answered Conner. "But we can't let the General know that he's alive. If he suspects the boy has told us what he heard, he may change his plans."

They arranged to meet at the Judicial Police Headquarters in Abidjan in the afternoon. When he put down the phone, Conner went to look for Roland and found him in his sitting room.

"I need you to come with me to Abidjan to press charges of theft against the General."

Roland stared into space for a moment and said, "No-can-do Conner. I'm sorry"

"But you have to," urged Conner. "Without a theft charge they can't prosecute the General. And we know he's been stealing from the mine."

"Don't you understand?" said Roland, dispirited with his head hung low. "I was in on it. I didn't realize it was on such a large scale, but I knew about the stealing and looked the other way. I was getting paid to look the other way. I should be in jail with him."

"You may have been an accomplice, but it was the General behind it. There's a big difference between masterminding and directing a theft ring and accepting a few bucks to look the other way. I'm sure the authorities will be happy to trade your testimony against the General for not pressing charges against you."

Roland was quiet a moment. He thought about Konaté's death and how much he wanted to keep it a secret. He thought about me, in a hospital bed with a concussion. He wished there was a way out.

"I'm sorry Conner. I can't do it. I feel terrible about what happened to Kwame and to you but if I press charges against the General and he gets off, my life won't be worth spit. And neither will yours. You know that's true because he already tried to do you in."

Conner considered explaining about the planned assassination and that it was necessary to get rid of the General once and for all or he would keep trying to overthrow the government but realized that Roland had no idea about the coup. He thought I was beaten because I found out about the gold theft. Conner didn't want any chance of the General finding out that the plan was no longer a secret that stopped with me.

"Fine, we'll do it without you. But just think about the value of your life if you don't do the right thing and help put him away," barked Conner. "It's going to take a lot of whiskey to wash away the guilt if more people murdered." He turned and stormed out of the room.

Lyla had her bag packed and was ready to go in a few minutes. They drove to Abidjan as quickly as possible and found the Judicial Police Headquarters. They were shown to a small meeting room on the second floor where Leon was sitting with a tired looking man who appeared to be in his early sixties eating a sandwich out of a paper bag and washing it down with coffee in a paper cup. He was wearing a white dress shirt with rolled up sleeves and a gun in a holster on his side. The room was hot and stuffy despite a noisy air-conditioning unit in the window that was fighting a losing battle.

"I'd like you to meet Chief Inspector Roger Koumassi," said Leon. "He's overseeing the investigation into the gold theft."

The inspector put down his food and rose to meet and shake hands with Conner and Lyla.

The inspector saw the bandages on Conner's wrists and asked what went on at the warehouse and how did Bamba end up dead.

Conner recounted the events while the inspector went back to his sandwich and coffee. When Conner finished, the Inspector shook his head. "Mr. Jackson. You are making my job extremely difficult," he said wiping the crumbs away from his mouth. "If it wasn't bad enough that you had to catch the Major General of the armed forces stealing gold and planning to overthrow the government, now one of his key staff has been electrocuted and shot in the head and you claim it was all in self-defense."

"Am I ever glad I don't have your job," laughed Conner.

There was a knock on the door and a well-dressed man about forty walked in carrying a briefcase. The Inspector introduced him as Mobio Kanga, the Prosecutor for the State. The Inspector pulled over another chair and Kanga joined them at the table. He proceeded to pull out a notepad and tape recorder.

"Thanks for making the trip to Abidjan today. It is of utmost importance that we have everything organized for our hearing tomorrow. We don't want any surprises or misunderstandings so I'm going to record our conversation and your statements and have our staff transcribe them. I will study them tonight and organize how we present our case. Where is Mr. Wells?"

"Unfortunately, he did not want to join us and has declined to press charges on behalf of Golden Sunshine Mining," explained Conner. "I think he is worried, as we all are, about possible reprisals from the General. Additionally, he appears to be hesitant to make a statement at the risk of incriminating himself."

"Is that so?" asked Kanga. "What was his involvement?"

"It appears that he was being paid to look the other way while the General stole gold from the mine."

It was quite apparent that this news was not what they wanted to hear as the Inspector and Kanga looked soberly at each other.

"Give us a moment," said Kanga as he and Koumassi got up and left the room.

They returned after a few minutes and Kanga said, "Please tell Mr. Wells that if he can see his way to testify against the General, and his involvement was limited to failure to report a theft, the State won't press charges against him. Perhaps that will help sway him to do the right thing."

"And if he still refuses?" asked Conner.

"Then we'll just have to do a better job of presenting the evidence and make it overwhelming enough to convince the Judge of the General's guilt," said Kanga. "If that's the case, the State can press charges."

Conner telephoned Roland explained that the Prosecutor had offered Roland immunity if he would testify against the General.

"What guarantee do I have that the General will even go to jail," asked Roland. "Immunity or not, it doesn't change the fact that if I testify against the General and he goes free, I'm done for."

"We're all in the same boat Roland. And all I can say for sure is that we'll have a better chance of putting him away if we stick together."

"I understand that Conner, but if the General found out I was testifying for the prosecution, I'd probably not even make it to court. I don't want to risk my own safety. And the risk is real. I hope you take Lyla's and your own safety into account. Good doesn't always triumph over evil."

When Conner hung up the phone, Kanga thanked him for trying and assured everyone that things would work out with or without Roland's cooperation. Then he turned on the tape recorder and Lyla made her statements regarding the calculations showing that there was gold missing. She explained how the carbon sacks were used to extract gold from the solution ponds and outlined the details of the altered refractory brick in the furnace. All the while, Kanga was jotting down notes and inquiring about details. When it was Conner's turn, he described how he slipped the monazite crystals into the slag bucket which was added to the pour to make the gold radioactive and thereby traceable. They had been at it for about an hour when the tape recorder clicked off and Kanga asked Conner to pause while he inserted a new blank tape. Leon verified that he had supplied the crystals and produced the Geiger counter.

"Well, I guess it's about time we tested this gold to see if it actually is radioactive," said the Inspector.

After the Inspector had left the room to retrieve the gold bar, Leon whispered to Conner, "I'm worried that the radioactivity won't have made it into the gold bar."

"Let me do the testing," Conner whispered back almost grabbing the instrument box out of Leon's hands as the Inspector returned with the gold bar and set it on the table. Conner unpacked the Geiger counter and turned it on.

"Here, let me," said Conner picking up the bar in his right hand and the sensor of the Geiger counter with his left.

He slowly moved the sensor, which was attached to the Geiger counter by a cable, back and forth over the bar. As the sensor was moved closer to the bar, the needle on the counter went up and a ticking sound was emitted from the main instrument. As it got closer, the ticking speeded up. When directly over the bar, the instrument ticked feverishly. He then handed the sensor to the inspector to repeat the test which gave the same result.

"I'd say that was pretty definitive," said Leon.

"For the benefit of the clerk transcribing this tape," stated Kanga, "let the record show that the Geiger counter reacted to the gold bar found in the possession of General Tiémoko. The bar is radioactive."

Conner put the gold bar back down on the table, turned off the Geiger counter and returned it to its case.

"I'll return this to the evidence vault," said the Inspector leaving with the gold bar.

When the inspector returned, Kanga continued asking questions and reviewing the facts. After they had been going at it for almost two hours Kanga said he had pretty well all he needed. He thanked everyone and reminded Lyla and Conner to be truthful under cross examination but not to offer any information that was not specifically requested.

They arranged to meet in the courtroom a few minutes before nine the next morning.

After Kanga had finished packing up and left, the Inspector explained that he had arranged to have the elite Tactical Assault Team hiding out at the Hotel Tiama the next morning to catch the "would be" assassin, and that the President's car would follow an alternate route just in case.

"The Team has orders to take the assassin alive, if at all possible, so we can interrogate him. Perhaps we could have him testify that the General was behind the operation. But it will be difficult because he may realize what we are trying to do. The words "stop or I'll shoot" don't mean much if he knows we won't shoot. We'll have the element of surprise on our side, but it will still be a long shot."

"Will you be involved in the operation?" asked Conner.

"Not directly. But I plan to watch from the periphery. Would you two care to join me?"

Conner and Lyla looked at each other and nodded.

"Fine, if you're finished in court before eleven o'clock, meet me here at the police station. After that, I'll be parked on the East side of Boulevard de le Republique near the Tiama in an unmarked car."

There wasn't much more they could do at the Police Headquarters, so Conner and Lyla left. It was getting dark and they checked into a hotel down the street. Later in the evening they met Leon for dinner.

After the drinks arrived, Leon said, "Thanks to the Spirits for helping Conner escape safely and seeing that the radioactivity was transferred into the gold bar," and he poured a little of his drink on the floor. "We can only hope that the Spirits will be with us in court tomorrow morning. We are going to need their help big time."

"What's the General saying in his defense?" asked Lyla. "How is he explaining where the gold came from?"

"He's not saying anything," answered Leon. "He's under no obligation to say anything until he goes to court. He and his lawyers are probably working out a plan."

The waiter came around and they all ordered their meals.

"So," Lyla summarized, "tomorrow's hearing is the key. If we can put away the General, the mine's problems and the President's problems are solved. But if he walks, a lot of things can go awfully wrong for all of us."

"That's an understatement," said Leon.

They continued chatting while they waited for their meals. Leon said to Conner, "Something has been nagging at me since this afternoon. Why were you so adamant about testing the gold for radioactivity yourself?"

Conner smiled and reached in his pocket producing a small monazite crystal. "I put them all in with the slag except this one," he said as he turned his hand palm up and stuck the crystal between two of his fingers so it couldn't be seen. He put a dinner roll on his hand and said, "If you waved a Geiger counter over this bun, I'll bet you could be convinced that the bun was radioactive."

"Did you learn that trick from your uncle the prospector?" asked Lyla.

"Let's just say, "The Spirits help those who help themselves," " answered Conner. They all laughed.

It was late by the time Conner and Lyla returned to their hotel. As they rode up in the elevator, Conner said, "I'm concerned about tomorrow. It would sure be nice to see the General locked up."

"Yes, there's a lot at stake," replied Lyla. "I hope for everyone's sake that it all works out."

When they got to their room Conner kicked off his shoes, lay down on the bed and turned on the TV. Lyla went and showered.

When she emerged from the bathroom she stood naked beside the bed. "I thought of something that might take your mind off tomorrow," she said.

Conner clicked off the remote and said, "I think it's working already."

Palais des Justice

Conner and Lyla arrived at the Palais des Justice courthouse at a quarter-to-nine to find Leon waiting near the main entrance. Once they passed through security and the metal detector, they were issued visitor's passes and directed to the proper courtroom. The three sat together behind the Prosecutor's table. Kanga came and conferred with them. He said he planned to call Lyla to the stand first and see how things went. If necessary, he would call Conner later.

"I'm nervous," said Lyla. "I've never been in a courtroom before, let alone on the witness stand."

"Don't worry," said Conner. "You'll be fine. You know your stuff inside-out."

"Tell that to my stomach. I wish I was back at the Chateau."

The courtroom filled up quickly and soon there were people standing against the back wall. Word had leaked that the General was being investigated and the press were all there hoping to hear a tale of greed and corruption. The courtroom was abuzz with speculation.

Shortly before nine the defense lawyer showed up. He was a tall, friendly looking Frenchman who wore a confident smile for all to see. His manner stated quite clearly that he had everything under control and his client had nothing to worry about.

Accompanying him were Roland and Jenny. He ushered Roland up to the Defense table at the front.

"What the hell?" muttered Conner. "Is he going to testify on behalf of the General?"

"I can't imagine what he could say that would help the General," said Lyla.

"They probably threatened to kill him if he didn't." said Leon as he looked up and saw Jenny walking toward the visitor's gallery. He waved her over and she came and joined them.

"What's going on Jenny?" asked Leon.

"The General had us brought to Abidjan last night. He said he needed Roland's help and there were no other options. Roland's got himself in a tough spot."

Roland didn't look around the courtroom, rather, he sat hunched over facing the front of the room.

The General strolled in and sat down with the defense counsel and Roland. He looked serious but almost a little cocky. He smiled and shook hands with Roland. Conner watched him as he conferred with the defense counsel and got organized. Then he started to look around the courtroom. First, he glanced at the Prosecutor's table and then the rest of the courtroom. He did a double take when he spotted Conner. Conner smiled at him and gave him a "thumbs up" sign.

The Judge came in and called the court to order. He had a round face and equally round body which couldn't be hidden by his black robes. His head was completely void of hair and sat atop his shoulders with no sign of a neck. Contrary to his gnomish appearance, he possessed a deep and resonating voice which easily captured the attention of the attendees.

"Welcome ladies and gentlemen. We are here today to listen to the Prosecutor for the State present evidence implicating Major General Anzoumana Tiémoko in an alleged gold theft conspiracy from the Abengourou Mine belonging to the Golden Sunshine Mining Company from Canada. The Defense will contest those charges and present their case as to the innocence of Major General Tiémoko. When both sides have completed their arguments, I will decide if there exists sufficient evidence to continue to a formal trial or to have the charges dropped."

"I would like to remind the court," the Judge continued, "that the Major General is an extremely busy man with an important job and his time is better spent overseeing the armed forces of our country rather than answering unsubstantiated charges. I will not permit any "hearsay" evidence to influence my decision or to defame the character of the defendant. And I remind the Defense that this court takes the laws of this land more seriously than you can imagine and although we are going to great lengths to ensure that your client gets a fair trial, the rank of the defendant will in no way influence the decision of his guilt or innocence. So please stick to the facts. Finally, I should remind the Press that however desperately you want a "sensational" story, releasing anything other than the facts may also make you liable. Anything else could land you back in this courtroom facing serious charges."

"I will now turn the floor over to the Prosecutor for the State to make his opening remarks."

"Thank you, Your Honor," began Kanga. "The engineering staff at the Abengourou Gold mine became aware that someone was stealing gold. They discovered where and how. The only question was who. They followed the gold as it was passed from hand to hand until on Saturday June 10, 1991, Major General Anzoumana Tiémoko, who owns private company that was contracted to oversee security at the mine, was arrested by the Judicial Police while carrying over four hundred ounces of gold into a gold trader's office just a few kilometers from the Mine. We have evidence proving that the gold came from the mine. It is clear, Your Honor, and we intend to demonstrate in this courtroom today, that the General was ultimately responsible for the theft and that formal charges should be laid."

"Thank you, counselor. The Defense can now proceed with its opening remarks."

The defense attorney rose, looked at the Prosecutor, and shook his head as if he was in disbelief.

"Your Honor, I really don't know where to start. But to be clear, the Defense would like to go on record by saying that we are extremely displeased with the actions of the Judicial Police and the Prosecutor's Office and that our client has been dealt a grave injustice."

"This is not the time nor place to be informing this court whether you are pleased or displeased," scolded the Judge. "This is your one opportunity to speak in defense of your client prior to this court deciding if it should levy formal charges against him. I don't want to have to explain this to you again," he said, raising his deep voice. "Have I made myself clear?"

"Yes, Your Honor, I'm sorry," replied the Attorney for the Defense. "I was just trying to explain that this whole thing is a misunderstanding. My client was carrying gold that was rightfully his. As the Prosecutor mentioned, a company controlled by Major General Tiémoko provides security services to the mine and the gold he was carrying was payment for those services. This entire fiasco could have been avoided simply by communicating through the proper channels and have saved the General an enormous amount of inconvenience and embarrassment. I suggest we stop this hearing immediately and save the participants a lot of time and the taxpayers a lot of money."

Conner, Lyla and Leon looked at each other in disbelief. Jenny just shook her head.

"Save the commentary for the locker room at the golf club Counselor," replied the Judge shaking his head. "You will be given ample opportunity to present proof of your claims. The hearing goes ahead. Do you have anything else to add?"

"No, Your Honor."

"Then let the Prosecution present its case."

"I would like to call as my first witness, Miss Lyla Townsend," said Kanga.

"Knock 'em dead," whispered Conner as Lyla got up and headed for the witness stand.

Once she was seated, the Prosecutor said, "Please state your name and occupation for the benefit of the court."

"Lyla Townsend. Process Plant Manager at the Abengourou Mine."

"Please state your credentials."

"I am a graduate of Mineral Process Engineering from the University of Melbourne," Lyla answered.

"Please explain, in your own words, how you became aware that someone was stealing gold from the Abengourou Mine."

"Well, at first all we knew was that there was a problem with the gold balance. According to my calculations, we should have been producing about five percent more gold than we were. So, we started checking for possible explanations. The Plant Production Engineer, Mamadou Toungara stayed late one evening to check on some ideas he had. His body was found later that night in one of the solution ponds with a significant contusion on the back of his head. It turned out that someone was hiding sacks of carbon in the solution pond to collect and steal the gold. Mamadou likely confronted the thieves and was murdered by them."

The Defense attorney jumped to his feet. "Objection Your Honor. That is speculation on the part of the witness."

"Sustained. Please stick to the facts Miss Townsend."

"What makes you think Mr. Toungara's death may have been other than accidental?" continued the Prosecutor.

"When I visited Dr. Kacou who performed the autopsy, he said he had ordered an x-ray to determine the severity of the contusion on Mamadou's head. To see if it was enough to render him unconscious. But the doctor was called away for a family emergency which turned out to be a hoax. While he was away, the body was cremated."

"So, what did you do when you eventually discovered the scheme?" asked the Prosecutor.

"I reported it to the Chief of Security and instituted a program whereby the Plant operators were to check each shift to make sure no carbon was hidden in the ponds."

"Was anyone held accountable for the theft?"

"No," answered Lyla. "It turned out that the security cameras didn't cover that area so there was no record or no way of knowing who was hiding the sacks."

"Please continue with your story Miss Townsend."

"Because we hadn't caught the thieves, we were suspicious that the gold theft might continue in a different way. So, we continued checking and found something peculiar in the furnace where the gold is melted. We confronted the plant operator that had been working on the furnace and asked him what was going on. All he said was, "He said they would kill our families if we didn't do as we were told."

"Who said they would kill their families?" asked the Prosecutor.

"We never found out. We planned to meet him privately on the weekend but instead he killed himself."

"He killed himself?"

"Yes. He went out in the jungle behind his house and slashed his wrists with a machete."

"So how did you find out what was going on?"

"We backed off and watched. When we saw the plant operator's assistant maintaining the furnace after the next pour, we watched, and he went directly to the Chief of Security's office. Then we saw the Operations Manager go to the same security office and leave with a heavy package. The Operations Manager met with the General that evening and the next morning the Judicial Police arrested General Tiémoko carrying a gold bar on his way into the gold trader's office."

"Thank you, Miss Townsend. The Prosecution has no more questions at this time."

The Prosecutor sat down, and the Judge said, "Does the defense have any questions for this witness?"

"Yes, Your Honor," said the Defense Attorney rising and approaching the witness box.

"Miss Townsend, you painted a pretty mysterious picture of the circumstances surrounding the Plant Production Engineer's death," said the Defense Attorney looking at his notes. "Surely there must have been some kind of autopsy or post mortem exam performed."

"Yes, there was. That's how the contusion was discovered."

"And what was the "Cause of Death" recorded on the death certificate?

"Drowning."

"Just "Drowning?" Nothing more?"

"Come to think of it, it said "Accidental Drowning." "

"Thank you, Miss Townsend. And did the Engineer say that he had an idea that someone was putting sacks of carbon in the ponds to steal gold and that he was going to try to catch them in the act?"

"No, he didn't."

"And did any of the security cameras show the presence of anyone other than the Engineer around the ponds that night?"

"No."

"Was it raining the night of the "Accidental Drowning" Miss Townsend?"

"Yes."

"Does the plastic liner material get slippery when wet?"

"Yes."

"So, in fact, isn't it quite possible that the Engineer had an idea of a completely different nature? Was out in the dark and the rain and slipped, banging his head on something and slipped into the pond and drowned?"

Lyla tried not to scowl at the Defense Attorney, knowing that he was trying to discredit her story.

"Please give me a yes or no answer Miss Townsend."

"Yes, I suppose."

"Thank you."

"Now, moving on. You said that you found something "peculiar" in the gold furnace. Please elaborate Miss Townsend."

"Actually, in the area with fresh grout between the refractory bricks, there was a small sharp point. Like the tip of a nail. Sometimes people steal gold by creating a void in the furnace liner. They use a nail, which will melt, to create a conduit to the void where the gold can be collected."

"Did you see a void?"

"No."

"Did you in fact see the Operator take a gold bar from the furnace?"

"No."

"Did you see him give it to the Chief of Security?"

"No."

"Did you see the Chief of Security give a gold bar to the Operations Manager?"

"No."

"Did you see the Operations Manager give a gold bar to the Major General?"

"No."

"So, everything between feeling the point of what might be a nail and the General being arrested with a gold bar is a guess?"

Lyla looked up at Conner and then at the Prosecutor. "I wouldn't call it a guess," said Lyla.

"Well you can call it what you want but I call it a colossal waste of the General's time. You may call yourself an engineer

Miss Townsend, but it seems to me that you're living in a fantasy world."

"Objection Your Honor," said the Prosecutor. "There is no need for the Defense Attorney to harass the witness."

"Objection sustained," said the Judge turning his attention toward the Defense Attorney. "This is the third time I've had to remind you to keep your commentary to yourself. Do it again and you will find yourself in contempt of court."

"Yes, Your Honor. I have no further questions for this witness."

"The witness may step down. Are there any more witnesses for the Prosecution?" asked the Judge.

"Yes, Your Honor. I would like to call Conner Jackson to the stand."

Conner made his way to the stand passing a sullen looking Lyla who was returning to her seat.

"Please state your name and occupation for the benefit of the court."

"My name is Conner Jackson and I am an Independent Mining Consultant doing a job for the mining company's underwriters."

"And your credentials?"

"I have a bachelor's and master's degree in Mining Engineering from Queen's University in Kingston, Canada."

"Mr. Jackson, please explain to the court the differences and similarities in gold bars produced by different mines," asked the Prosecutor.

"Gold is gold. Element 79 on the periodic table. But gold bars produced at mines generally contain impurities. Most commonly silver. Often copper. It depends on the metallurgical process used and the mineralogical makeup of the ore. Doré bars, as they are called, would generally run between fifty and eighty percent gold."

"Would an analysis of the doré bar be a definitive indicator of the mine from which it originated?"

"Not normally," explained Conner. "Unless there was some unique mineral in the ore which made its way to the gold bar, there would be no way of telling with any level of confidence."

"Then would you please explain to the court how it is that the Chief Inspector of the Judicial Police signed this affidavit saying that testing of the gold, or rather, doré bar, that was found in the possession of General Tiémoko, showed that it came from the Abengourou Mine?"

"I introduced a mildly radioactive mineral, monazite, into the slag which was added to the gold in the furnace. The bar in the General's possession tested positive for radioactivity using a Geiger counter."

"Thank you. No further questions Your Honor."

"Would the defense care to cross-examine the witness?" inquired the Judge.

"Yes, we would Your Honor."

"Mr. Jackson," said the Defense Attorney, "Please tell the court how it was that Miss Townsend discovered the sacks of carbon in the solution pond."

"We were visiting the mine for another reason and decided to observe the ponds in the late evening. Around the same time of night that the Operations Engineer had his accident. We hid in a storage shed and watched and waited until two men wearing army fatigues came through the fence behind the ponds. They removed two sacks from the ponds and put two more in."

"Did you ask them what they were doing?"

"Not likely. We didn't want to end up on the bottom of the pond like the Operations Engineer."

"Just answer the questions please Mr. Jackson," said the Defense Attorney. "So, what did you do about it?"

"That was Saturday night. We waited until Monday morning and Miss Townsend pretended to find the sacks by accident."

"Why didn't you report the security breach immediately? Surely Miss Townsend's superior would have wanted to be informed."

"Her superior was Adjobi Konaté, the Operations Manager. He was in on the scheme. As guilty as the rest."

"How can you be so sure? If he was a suspect, why isn't he in court today?"

"He disappeared around the same time as the General was arrested. I don't think he's coming back," added Conner.

"Why didn't you tell the Chief of Security? Surely that would be the protocol when someone sees a theft in process."

"Again, rotten, crooked and in on it."

"Mr. Jackson. I'll ask you to refrain from passing judgement on guilt and innocence until the person has had an opportunity to defend themselves."

"Won't happen," said Conner.

"Why not?"

"He died yesterday."

"How," asked the Defense Attorney.

The courtroom went quiet at everyone listened intently.

"He was trying to shoot me, and someone shot him in the head."

"Why on earth, Mr. Jackson," asked the Attorney, "would he be trying to shoot you?"

"He was probably mad because I electrocuted him."

The courtroom, which was almost silent up to this point, erupted into a din of gasping, conversation and some outright laughter.

The Judge pounded his gavel and told the court to be quiet. He interrupted the questioning and asked the Prosecutor if he was aware of these events. The Prosecutor assured him that the Chief Inspector was aware and dealing with the case.

"How convenient Mr. Jackson," continued the Defense Attorney, "that two of the key players you are accusing as accomplices to General Tiémoko, aren't able to present a defense."

"No further questions Your Honor."

The Judge asked if the Prosecution had any further witness to call to the stand, but Kanga declined.

"Let the Defense call its first witness."

"The Defense calls Mr. Roland Wells to the stand."

If Roland felt as poorly as he looked, he was to be pitied. His clothes were wrinkled, his hair was messy, his eyes were bloodshot and his hands were shaking.

"Please state your name and occupation for the benefit of the court," said the Defense Attorney.

"Roland Wells, General Manager of the Abengourou Mine, said Roland with his voice quivering as badly as his hands were shaking.

"Mr. Wells, please explain your arrangement with the General regarding payment for security services."

"What do you mean?" asked Roland.

The Defense Attorney gave Roland a questioning look and said, "Please explain to the court that the gold the General was carrying was payment for services under the mine security contract."

Roland took a deep breath and looked around the courtroom. His eyes met Jenny's and he nodded his head. "That's entirely untrue," he said. "The fact is that the General was stealing gold from the mine."

The Assassin

The General jumped to his feet. "Shut the hell up you idiot," he yelled.

"Order in the Court!" shouted the Judge. "One more outbreak and I'll have you removed from the courtroom General."

The room went quiet. "Please continue Mr. Wells," instructed the Judge angrily.

"The defense has no further questions for this witness Your Honor," said the Defense Attorney realizing that Roland had done an "about face."

"Then the Prosecution shall have an opportunity to question the witness," responded the Judge.

The Prosecutor rose and said, "Please continue Mr. Wells."

"I was in on it. I was to look the other way while the General's staff stole the gold. I was getting a cut. We were stealing from the mining company."

"How long has this been going on?" asked the Prosecutor.

"Over a year."

"And how much gold do you estimate has been stolen?"

"Several million dollars' worth."

"Are you one hundred percent certain that General Tiémoko was behind this?" interrupted the Judge. "The General holds the highest-ranking position in the Armed Forces of the Ivory

Coast. We don't want to get into a frivolous case that could hurt his reputation."

"Completely certain Your Honor. But that's not the worst of it. It was brought to my attention recently that his people did kill the Plant Operations Engineer who discovered them stealing gold," said Roland. "They knocked him unconscious and drowned him in a cyanide pond."

"Objection Your Honor!" shouted the Defense Attorney. "Hearsay. There is no evidence. The death certificate said, "Accidental drowning."

Kanga stood and said, "The prosecution requests permission to approach the bench Your Honor."

Kanga and the Defense Attorney walked up to the Judge's bench and the Prosecutor lowered his voice and addressed the Judge, "Your Honor, this hearing was intended to determine if there were sufficient evidence to levy charges of theft against General Tiémoko. It has become apparent that there is a lot more going on than we anticipated. I would like to request a recess pending an investigation by the Judicial Police during which time the defendant remain in custody."

"Defense? Any comment?"

"Yes, Your Honor. This is ridiculous. Mr. Wells must be confused. Earlier today he told me there was no theft. Now he says the complete opposite. He's obviously unstable and his testimony should not be taken seriously. My client is an important man and his job is critical to the security of our Country. You have no evidence and mustn't detain him based on the ravings of a lunatic."

"Remember this so called "lunatic" is your witness," said the Judge. "That being said, we won't detain your client based solely on comments made by a witness. A recommendation from the Judicial Police following a full investigation and consultation with the Prosecutor's Office will be required to decide if anyone is to be detained."

The Judge addressed the court, "This hearing will be adjourned for two weeks or until a full investigation has been completed. In the meantime, General Tiémoko will be released on his own recognizance." He pounded his gavel on the bench, stood and left the courtroom through the private entrance.

The reporters crowded around the General as he made his way to the exit. Roland made his way over to the rest of the group and they each expressed their surprise at the sudden turn of events.

"What the hell just happened?" asked Conner.

"We all just got added to the General's shit list," replied Roland. "And he's been allowed to go free."

The Prosecutor stepped over to the group and said. "Sorry guys. That really didn't go the way I wanted."

"Don't worry," said Leon. "The Judicial Police are on our side. They want to nail the General as badly as we do. We can help them with their investigation and put an airtight case together."

"Do you think the Judge was paid off?" asked Lyla to no one in particular.

"Could be," replied the Prosecutor. "If that's the case we have our work cut out for us. But it will help having Mr. Wells on our side. Thanks, by the way, for doing the right thing."

"I must have had a weak moment," said Roland shaking his head.

"Can you come by the Judicial Police Headquarters this afternoon to make a statement?" the Prosecutor asked Roland.

Roland agreed, and they arranged to meet after lunch.

Leon said he had to rush off to the National Assembly building because Parliament was still in session and he could at least catch the end of the day's activity.

It was almost noon, so Conner and Lyla went to meet Inspector Koumassi as previously arranged.

It was only about four blocks from the Palais des Justice to the Tiama Hotel. Conner and Lyla walked down Boulevard de Republique until they spotted the Inspector sitting in a car across from the hotel.

The Inspector was eating a croissant from a paper bag and drinking take-out coffee. They got in the car with him. The midday sun was beating down and even with all the windows open, the heat was oppressive. They filled the Inspector in on the outcome of the hearing.

"I was afraid this would happen. I'll bet he either bribed or threatened the Judge," said the Inspector. "It's going to be incredibly difficult to put him behind bars."

The Tactical Assault Team had been sent to the Tiama Hotel at ten o'clock to wait for the assassin.

It was shortly after noon when the chatter started on the radio.

"*There was a man with a suitcase entering the hotel and heading directly for the elevators instead of the front desk.*"

"*Getting off the elevator at the top floor.*"

"*Suspect heading for the stairway to the roof.*"

"*Suspect in custody. Repeat. Suspect in custody. Bringing him to the lobby.*"

"Wow, that was easy," said Lyla. "Not a shot fired."

They watched as the Assault team van pulled up in front of the hotel and two armed personnel stepped out and walked up to the front door of the hotel.

As the elevator doors opened, the suspect, who had his hands cuffed behind his back, managed to knock the guard holding his arm off balance and bolt into the lobby yelling "Shoot them!"

A man, who must have been the assassin's lookout, had been sitting in an armchair pretending to read the newspaper, jumped up and took cover behind the large pillar. He started firing a revolver at the two escorting guards by the elevator who started firing back. The two personnel from the truck were about to walk into the main entrance when the shots erupted, and they jumped back just as the suspect flew out the door. Amongst the shooting and people screaming, they were unable to decide if they should pursue the suspect or help their colleagues.

One stayed to help and the other, under strict instructions that the suspect should be taken alive, started running after the suspect who by now had crossed the busy Boulevard. As the team member also made his way across the Boulevard chasing the suspect, he called in on his radio, "*Suspect has escaped. Heading east on foot along Rue Jesse Owens.*"

The Inspector, Conner and Lyla heard the shots and watched the events unfold in a matter of seconds.

The suspect was running like the wind and lengthening the gap between himself and his clumsy Tactical Assault Team assailant clad in helmet, bullet proof vest and boots and his machine gun bouncing against his side.

All three jumped out of the car and Conner and Lyla started running down the street behind the Team member. The Inspector shouted, "You have to wait here." But neither Conner nor Lyla listened. The inspector got in his car and maneuvered it around so he could follow the quickly disappearing suspect. It didn't take long for Conner and Lyla to pass the Tactical Assault Officer, but the fleeing villain moved at an incredible speed.

Even though the plan was to take the suspect alive, bringing him back dead or wounded would be better than not bringing him back at all. If it looked as if the suspect were escaping, the protocol was to shoot. Conner and Lyla heard the Officer shout at them to get down so he could fire at the suspect, but they kept right on chasing him.

After three blocks, the street turned south, however, the suspect crashed straight through a hedge and disappeared. Lyla, now well ahead of Conner followed at top speed. When she emerged from the bushes she saw the suspect going through an open door in a concrete block wall on the other side of a lawn. She sprinted as fast as she could and when she reached the other side of the wall, found that she was in the parking area of a gas station beside the Boulevard de Gaulle. On the other side of the Boulevard was the shore of Abidjan Harbor.

The suspect raced through the three lanes of southbound traffic with Lyla gaining on him. As they crossed the grass dividing median, she spotted a speed boat with two armed personnel at the water's edge about fifty meters away. They were obviously waiting for the assassin because as soon as they saw he was being chased, they jumped into action, raising their machine guns.

Halfway across the northbound lanes, Lyla caught up to the fleeing fugitive and kicked her foot in between his to trip him. With his hands behind his back, he had no way to protect himself and hit the pavement hard. Lyla lost her balance and landed on top of him. Traffic on the Boulevard came to a screeching halt. The suspect struggled to get to his feet, but with his hands behind his back and Lyla on top of him, it was impossible.

Conner arrived with the Tactical Assault Officer close behind him. The men on the boat started firing in their direction but the Officer returned the fire. Realizing there was nothing they could do; the accomplices took off in their boat. Inspector Koumassi arrived with siren blaring and lights flashing as two more Tactical Assault Officers arrived on foot. Koumassi put in a call to the dispatcher to alert the marine unit of the fleeing boat. They hauled the suspect off the road so the traffic could get by and the tactical assault van arrived soon after to pick him up.

The Inspector pulled the suspect to his feet and grabbing the front of his shirt said, "Who hired you?"

The suspect just grinned at the Inspector. His teeth all bloodied from hitting the pavement.

"Cuff his ankles too so he doesn't try running away again," ordered the inspector.

The Tactical team put shackles on the suspect's ankles with a chain going up to his handcuffs. As they were loading him into the van, the inspector said, "I'll see you back at the station my little friend. You and I have a lot to talk about."

"Nice takedown," Conner said to Lyla as the van drove off.

"Just a little something I learned from my uncle the soccer player," replied Lyla looking quite proud of herself. "It's a good thing one of us stays in shape."

"Damn right," laughed Conner. "I figured you must play dirty to do so well."

The inspector explained that they would be needed at Headquarters one more time for paperwork relating to the arrest.

Conner asked, "Do you think you'll be able to get him to admit that he was hired by the General?"

"That shouldn't be much trouble considering his alternative could be life in prison or the death penalty if we convict him of treason," the Inspector explained. "Ivorian jails are not what you would call inviting. Virtually one hundred per cent of the inmates have aids and malaria after one year. A life sentence doesn't last too long here."

They rode back to the station with the inspector and made their formal statements regarding the arrest of the suspect. As they were leaving the building, they ran into Roland and Jenny who were on their way in.

Conner said, "Thanks for doing what you did today. Standing up to the General like that. I know how difficult it must have been."

"It doesn't seem to have helped much," answered Roland. "But it had to be done. I'm coming in now to make my statement for the record."

"When will you be heading back to the Chateau?" asked Lyla.

"Well, here's the thing. I'm not," answered Roland. "Jenny and I are leaving for England tonight. Time to pack up and retire. We'll send for the rest of our things."

"That's awfully sudden," said Conner.

"Yes, but we don't want to hang around waiting for repercussions from my testimony against the General. And, I think it's best for me to get out of here in case the Prosecutor's office changes its mind about not pressing charges against me."

"Who's running things at the mine?" asked Lyla.

"I put Michael Vandoorn in charge. He's not happy about taking on the job but he'll keep things afloat until the Golden Sunshine finds my replacement. I sent in my resignation to the head office about an hour ago."

"We are going to miss you guys," said Jenny hugging both Conner and Lyla.

"Please say goodbye to Kwame for us. Tell him to visit us on his world travels," added Roland.

They wished each other luck and Conner and Lyla headed back to their hotel.

Leon called later that afternoon.

"Inspector Koumassi told me what happened today," he told Conner over the phone. "He says he wants to recruit Lyla for the Tactical Assault Team."

"Sorry, she's already signed up with the Ivorian soccer team," quipped Conner.

"He'll be disappointed, but he asked me to pass on some news to you both. The assassin has delivered a sworn statement saying that he was hired by the General to assassinate President Bakayoko. The Prosecutor has gone to the Supreme Court seeking approval to formally charge the General with treason."

"A lot of people are going to sleep better once he's been taken off the streets," said Conner.

"That's for sure," Leon agreed. "Oh, and Conner, the Prosecutor asked if you and Lyla wouldn't mind sticking around Abidjan for a couple of days? Until we get this mess sorted out? You may be required to answer more questions."

"No problem Leon. Anything that will help put the General where he belongs."

Feeding Time

Iwas recovering rapidly and by Monday was starting to get restless. My mother was pleased to see this and left the hospital around mid-day to tend to things at home. Boredom was starting to set in when I was pleasantly surprised to have a visit from Nsia. I still had a large bandage wrapped around my head and Nsia flinched a little when she saw it. She told me that everyone at the Chateau were worried about me, so she decided to come and see for herself what was going on.

When I told her that I was scheduled to be released from the hospital Tuesday, she said, "Then we can expect you back at work Wednesday?"

"I'm sorry Nsia, but the doctor told me to stay home for the rest of the week."

"Well you look fine to me but if the doctor insists, there's not much I can do about it," said Nsia sternly. "Just make sure you come back in good shape Monday. The rest of us can't be carrying your load forever. I'm getting tired of feeding the goat and monkey and I need you to put some things away on the high shelf."

I noticed her pull out a tissue and wipe something from her eye before she came over to my bedside, patted my shoulder and left without another word.

I was released from the hospital Tuesday morning. My mother and I rode the bus back to my village. My friends and family were all there to greet me. They had only been told the official story about my accident. The one Roland told when he first brought me unconscious to emergency. They all thought I had been walking into Abengourou from the Chateau and had been beaten and robbed. I told everyone I couldn't remember but they asked for details anyway. Some asked if I had done something to annoy the Spirits. Perhaps I had. All I knew for sure was that I was just glad to be home.

I was feeling great though I still had a bit of a lump on the back of my head. The doctor had issued strict instructions that I wasn't to play soccer for at least a week. I was to take it easy and spend time with my family. Everything was going great until my father came home. He asked me to go for a walk with him and off we went around the soccer field.

"It's good to have you home Kwame. We missed you and worried about you. But now that you have recovered, it's time for you to tell me what really happened that night."

I thought of trying to pretend that I didn't know what he was talking about but realized that wasn't going to get me anywhere. He was too smart for that and could tell when I was lying. I knew he wasn't going to be pleased but I went ahead and told him the truth. When I finished, we walked silently for some time.

Finally, he said, "You defied my wishes that you stay out of other people's business. But you may have saved our President's life and our Country from being taken over by a terrible man. You did what you felt you had to, and that's all any man can do. And I'm glad you made it home safely. Now let's go home and enjoy that nice dinner your mother has prepared."

Before we ate my father thanked the Spirits for the food and for returning me safely home.

After dinner I collected some scraps and walked over to the rescue center to visit Okwan. When I saw he wasn't in his enclosure I asked the vet where he was.

"We released him into the Sanctuary a couple of days ago. I don't think he's gone too far. We found a mate for him in a sanctuary in the north and want him to get accustomed to being back in the wild before she arrives next week. Try calling him."

I called and waited and watched through the dim light filtering into the jungle. A horrible thought passed through my head that perhaps he was gone, and I hadn't had a chance to say goodbye when I saw two glowing yellow eyes appear in the shadows. There was Okwan on the other side of the fence. He came over to me and I passed the food through the opening. My friend still remembered me.

Conner and Lyla stuck close to their hotel the next day hoping to hear some news from Leon.

They ate lunch in the hotel restaurant and when they returned to their room the message light on the phone was flashing. Leon had called so Conner called him back.

"I hope you were calling to tell me the General is behind bars," said Conner.

"I'm sorry my friend but I have a bit of bad news. The Prosecutor presented the testimony of the assassin to the Supreme Court Judge, but the Defense Attorney argued that because the accused was testifying in return for receiving immunity, he would have been willing to point the finger at anyone. The Judge wasn't prepared to file charges based on that testimony alone."

"That's ridiculous," Conner protested. "We knew where the assassin was going to be and waited for him. We must have overheard the General detailing his plans or how would we know about it."

"That's exactly what the Prosecutor argued but the Judge was adamant that first hand testimony would be required. He said that he wants Kwame to be brought in to testify himself. And the Defense Attorney insisted on being given an opportunity to cross-examine. The hearing has been scheduled for Friday to give the Judicial Police a chance to bring Kwame to Abidjan tomorrow."

"I don't like where this is headed," said Conner. "It doesn't appear that the Judge wants to put the General away. We catch the General red-handed with $160,000 worth of stolen gold, the mining company presses charges and the Judge says he wants an investigation." Conner's voice was getting louder, and Lyla was listening and shaking her head. Conner continued, "We catch the assassin in the act and he testifies that he was hired by the General to fire a missile at the President's car. And what does the Judge do? He says he wants to hear from the boy. Christ almighty Leon, I think the Judge has been compromised and the General is going to walk; no matter what anyone testifies."

"I know it looks that way Conner, but there must be a way. I'll talk to the President. Perhaps he needs to have a talk with the Judge."

"That might work if the Judge was more afraid of the President than the General, but I wouldn't count on it."

"Don't give up Conner. We'll figure out how to put the General away," assured Leon. "Oh, and one more thing I thought I should tell you. Both the Prosecutor and Inspector Koumassi mentioned to me that the General asked them where you and Lyla were staying. Neither of them knew so he likely didn't find out. But I would keep a low profile if I were you. The Inspector offered to assign someone to keep an eye on you if you'd like."

"That shouldn't be necessary," answered Conner. "But I'll let you know if we need anything."

"Okay my friend. Take Care."

Conner put down the phone shaking his head and related the details of the conversation to Lyla.

"I agree with you Conner. I don't like where this is headed. I know Leon is your friend and you want to do everything you can to help him, but we don't seem to be making any progress. Perhaps it's time to cut our losses and get out of here."

"I'm afraid to say I think you're right. At least until things settle down one way or another. I'm going to talk to the agent at the travel desk in the lobby and see if there are any flights out of here today."

Conner went to his suitcase and dug out the pistol he had taken from Bamba. Handing it to Lyla he asked, "Do you know how to use one of these?"

"Of course," said Lyla opening the revolver to make sure it was loaded. My father wouldn't let me go to the outback without one. Never know when you might be prey for a pack of hungry dingoes," Lyla laughed.

"Well I don't think we need to worry about any dingoes here. But it would be good to keep it close in case the General decides to pay us a visit. Keep the chain on the door," said Conner closing it behind himself.

While she was waiting for Conner to return, Lyla packed her suitcase in anticipation of their departure. Leon's comment had made her nervous and Conner seemed to be taking an extremely long time. She tried to occupy her mind with other things but checked her watch every few minutes. After more than an hour, a knock came on the door. She looked through the security hole and was relieved to see Conner in the hallway.

"Sorry to take so long. They made me wait while a courier brought the tickets over from the airlines office. Two one-way tickets to Paris leaving tonight at six-thirty," he said holding up the tickets. "We should head to the airport around four o'clock."

"That's wonderful. I'm so relieved. I think we're doing the right thing. If they put the General away, we'll come back. If not, it's better we aren't around."

While Conner packed his bag he said, "I feel bad about leaving Kwame on his own. It was me who asked him to spy on the General and I won't be around when he has to testify."

"That's unfortunate," agreed Lyla. "But the Judicial Police will take care of him. Pick him up and bring him back home. And Leon will be there. He knows Leon."

Conner continued packing and then he froze. "Wait just a minute. Something Leon said has been bothering me and I just figured out why."

"What's that?" asked Lyla.

"He said that the Defense Attorney insisted on being given an opportunity to cross-examine Kwame."

"So?"

"The fact that Kwame is the witness was supposed to be a secret. Don't you see? The Defense Attorney now knows that Kwame was the witness. And if the Defense Attorney knows, so does the General. And he knows that Kwame's testimony is key. What's to stop the General from getting rid of Kwame?"

"Oh my god Conner. We've got to do something. If the General is prepared to kill the President to get what he wants, he probably wouldn't think twice about killing Kwame. I think we should go and get Kwame right now."

"I think you're right. We could take Kwame to the Chateau for the night and bring him in to Abidjan tomorrow. At least we would know he's safe."

Conner put the gun in his bag and as they left the hotel through the lobby, Conner dropped the plane tickets on the agent's deck and asked her to change them to tomorrow's flight.

"Let me drive," said Conner as they climbed in Lyla's truck, and headed for Abengourou as fast as they could.

Unfortunately, rush hour had started, and the traffic was terrible. They were in the south end of the city and the highway to Abengourou exited the city from the north. That meant they had to cross the entire city before getting away from the stop and go traffic. Crowded busses were blowing black diesel smoke at them as they cut into traffic. Intersections were blocked with cars stopped in all directions and angry drivers were honking and yelling at each other. Just when it looked like they were going to be stuck for hours, and ambulance went by heading north. Conner pulled out behind it and followed directly on its bumper. It wasn't speeding but was moving a lot faster than any other cars were going.

Lyla looked at Conner and said, "What the hell are you doing?"

"Just a little trick I learned in Jamaica," Conner said with a grin.

By the time the ambulance turned off their route, they were almost out of the city.

I was eating dinner with my family when an army jeep pulled up in front of our house. A uniformed soldier got out, stopped a neighbor passing by and asked him something. The neighbor pointed at our house.

"Do you know what's going on Kwame?" my father asked me.

"No, but that looks like the General."

"I want you to go quickly out the back door and run and hide. Go now!"

As the General was walking toward the front door, I slipped out the back. My siblings and mother gazed at each other dumbfounded. The General knocked on the door and as my father rose to answer he gave them all a sign to button their lips.

"How can I help you?" asked my father.

"I would like to talk with Kwame Kouassi," said the General.

"For what reason?" inquired my father.

"I have a warrant for his arrest."

"On what charges?"

"For interfering with military operations," said the General looking around the room.

"I'm sure there must be some mistake," said my father. "Kwame would never interfere with anything."

"Enough. Where is he?"

"He's not here. He went to visit a cousin in the north of the country."

The General spotted the empty seat at the table. He grabbed my younger brother's arm who had been seated beside me and yelled, "Where is your brother?"

My brother's eyes filled with tears, his mouth opened but nothing but a loud wail came out.

He must have spotted the door leading outside through the back of the kitchen because he started moving in that direction.

"Get out of my house!" shouted my father stepping in front of the General and pushing him back.

"Don't touch me," said the General pulling out his sidearm.

My father grabbed his wrist but the General managed to get off a shot and my father fell backwards onto the floor. The General stepped over him and rushed out through the back door.

I was running down the street as fast as I could when the shot rang out. I stopped for a second and turned around. My father didn't own a firearm, so I could only assume that the General had fired the shot. Had my father been killed? I considered going back to help but saw the General come out from behind our house. He spotted me, and I took off again.

I had no idea where I was going. The best thing would be to head into the jungle but by this point, I had reached the fence enclosing the Wildlife Sanctuary preventing me from entering. So, I kept running. Then I realized that if I kept going straight, I would end up at the mine which was full of the General's men and I'd be caught for certain.

Then it struck me. "The Animal Rehabilitation Facility had an entrance to the Sanctuary." I would use that. The entrance was about two hundred meters ahead and I was moving fast. I knew there was no way the General could catch me. I was going to get away. I took a quick look over my shoulder to see how much distance I had on the General and saw that he was in his jeep. Barreling toward me at top speed.

My lungs were burning but I kept running as fast as I could. I knew I had to beat him to the Sanctuary. I could hear the jeep bearing down on me. The entrance was just ahead. Would he try to run me down or cut me off? I soon found out as he skidded sideways in front of me, blocking the entrance to the Facility. As he was getting out of the jeep I flew over the hood and kept running toward the entrance to the Sanctuary.

The entrance was a chain link fence gate, eight feet high. As I reached it and lifted the latch, I heard the General shout, "Stop or I'll shoot."

I knew he meant it. But I figured if he caught me he would kill me anyway. So, I opened the gate enough to squeeze through and continued running. I heard a shot and the sound of a ricochet off the steel gate frame.

"Okwan," I yelled. "Okwan."

In a matter of seconds, the General was through the gate and fired another shot that hit a tree beside me. I figured my luck had just about run out when I heard Okwan roar. I don't know if it was the sound of the gunshot that triggered his memory of his experience being shot by the poachers or if his hunting instinct took over, but I turned around to see him landing on the General. The General screamed as he hit the ground and Okwan sunk his huge teeth into the back of his neck. The gun went flying as he shook the General's head back and forth like a rag doll until the screaming stopped. His neck was most certainly broken. Then he ripped the flesh from the General's arm and leapt up in the tree where he ate it hungrily.

I walked slowly past the General's body, which had the bone of his arm exposed and bloody, went out the gate and closed it behind me. I could see down the road that a group of people had gathered in front of our house. I ran as fast as I could, praying that the Spirits had not taken my father. I arrived to find my father being loaded into the back seat of a car to be taken to the hospital. There was blood everywhere. My father was conscious and in terrible pain. My mother was crying and all I could think of was that it was all my fault.

Conner and Lyla arrived a few minutes later and were over-joyed to see that I was okay. I told them what happened, and although they were upset about my father, they were pleased to hear the news of the General's death. Conner said he would call and report the events to the Inspector. I distracted Okwan while Conner and the vet dragged what was left of the General's body out the Sanctuary gate and covered it with a sheet for the Judicial Police to recover.

They operated on my father that night and the surgeon said that despite all the blood and pain, no internal organs were damaged. The bullet made a clean exit and my father was expected to experience a full and hasty recovery. The Spirits had been watching over him.

Presidential Palace

Early one morning, about a week later, I was in the garden feeding the goat and monkey when Conner came to me and said, "President Bakayoko is arranging a ceremony, to be held in at the Presidential Palace, in honor of the people who contributed to thwart the attempted assassination and coup. Lyla and I will be going, and he requested that you attend as well."

"The President?" I said. "What does he want me there for? I've never even been to Abidjan. I wouldn't know what to do or say."

"Don't worry Kwame. Lyla and I will be with you the whole time. We can drive down in the morning and back in the afternoon. It'll be fine."

Konaté's body, or what was left of it, was found on a beach near the mouth of the river. What the crocodiles and fish hadn't consumed was being picked at by the vultures and beach crabs. There was no way to, or no one wanted to, determine cause of death. The one remaining hand sported a huge gold ring.

Conner and Lyla returned to Abidjan with me for the ceremony at the Presidential Palace. I was fully recovered but started wondering if I was still dreaming as we were ushered through the Palace gates.

Leon greeted us and introduced us to President Bakayoko.

"When are you heading back to Canada?" Leon asked Conner.

"Actually, I have accepted the job of General Manager at the mine. I thought I would take a page out of your book and settle down a bit," Conner said as he reached for Lyla's hand.

"Well, you won't regret it. I'm so happy for you my friend. You two make a great couple."

There were a lot of dignitaries and friends of the President at the reception. He truly wanted to show everyone his gratitude. He made a speech explaining the events that led up to the arrest and finally the demise of the General, including my eavesdropping, Conner's knowledge of gold stealing, Lyla's quick footedness, Piesie's bravery, the Inspector's perseverance and Michael Vandoorn's keen observation and marksmanship. He also explained that he was grateful not only for himself, but for his country and all its citizens including everyone present, that the General didn't take over and create a dictatorship. He was so moved, he had tears in his eyes when he turned and presented us with commemorative medals and asked us to say a few words.

Conner grabbed the microphone first. "Just doing my job," he said. "Glad it all worked out," he added as he stepped down. He lowered the microphone stand for Lyla.

Lyla looked a bit nervous speaking in front of all those people but managed to say, "I just couldn't resist showing the guy that I could run faster than him. Thank you President Bakayoko. We really don't deserve all this attention."

Then it was my turn. I stepped up to the microphone and opened my mouth, but nothing came out. My knees got weak and I thought I might faint. The President could see I was having trouble and walked over and put his arm around my shoulder.

"Just tell us why you did what you did. Why did you help, Kwame?"

"I don't know, I just did. It seemed like the right thing to do."

"Then please tell me Kwame, how can I repay you?"

I thought a few seconds and replied, "I would really like to finish high school."

"Well, we can certainly arrange that. And perhaps a university education overseas, like Minister Djedje"

"Mr. President, there is nothing I would like more but my family can't afford it."

"Don't worry. I'll pay for it. It's the least I can do for someone who saved my life."

The audience clapped and cheered.

"Well," I thought, "the Spirits are certainly smiling on me today."

When I returned to my village, I told my father about the President's offer. I was afraid he would forbid me to leave and was prepared to be disappointed. Instead he said "Kwame, I believe your destiny lies outside our small village and you should follow your heart. Go and make us proud. And remember we'll always be here should you want to return."

And so it was, that I went to a boarding school in London to finish my high school diploma and then continued on to a fine arts degree in music at university. Jenny and Roland were the only people I knew in the country at the beginning and were a tremendous support. They let me stay with them on holidays and were always eager to help in any way over the years. I spent a year as an exchange student in Poland which is where I met Sofiya. We were married after I finished my teaching degree. It was a lot of work and I always had a part time job to contribute as much as I could. But the generosity of President Bakayoko and the profitability of his cacao plantations made it possible.

London 2017

Epilogue

And that's the story of what happened in the Ivory Coast all those years ago. And how I ended up in England. I don't know if the Spirits played any part in it, or care for that matter. Although I believe the Spirits of the dead live on, I have long stopped attributing life's ups and downs to their whims.

I was able to track down Conner and Lyla, who were key, along with Jenny, in filling in the details of this story. They married and stayed on at the mine for five years. Lyla continued Jenny's work with new mothers at the Nouvel Espoir post-natal clinic. After their first daughter was born, they moved to Argentina where their second daughter was born. The couple now spends half their time in Canada and the other half sailing in the Caribbean on their forty-foot yacht.

As it seems to happen in the Ivory Coast, this was not the last, nor second last coup attempt on the President's administration. His government was finally overthrown several years later, and he fled to France where he lives today.

The mine at Abengourou has long since been exhausted and closed. The mine site was decommissioned, and the land added to the Sanctuaire de Faune de l 'or. The jungle in the mine area has almost completely grown back to the way it was before the project was started. The sanctuary still thrives today.

Once it was no longer needed, the Golden Sunshine Mining Company donated Chateau Abengourou to Jenny's foundation as the new home of the Nouvel Espoir clinic which has grown and has helped thousands of new mothers and their babies. And each year, Sofiya and I make a donation in memory of my two "gone but not forgotten" siblings.

Acknowledgements

I WOULD LIKE TO THANK THE FOLLOWING people for their help and advice in the preparation of SPIRITS' GOLD:

Cathleen Condren
David Paterson
Maureen Paterson
Michael Paterson
Norman B. Paterson
Norman R. Paterson
Sally Paterson
Michael Sabo

About the Author

My career as a mining engineer took me to 5 continents searching for and developing gold, diamond and base metal mines. In 2006, my wife Maureen and I moved from our home near Toronto to southern Costa Rica where we now own and operate a small nature lodge and coffee farm (Rio Magnolia). Our property is off-grid, where we generate their own electricity with a micro hydro plant and protect 200 acres of rain and cloud forest. We host nature enthusiasts, wildlife photographers and other assorted characters from around the world.

As an engineer, I enjoyed writing reports and technical papers but never tried my hand at fiction. I've always loved reading, especially authors like John Grisham, Robert B. Parker and Andy Weir among many others. In 2016, after taking some online courses I wrote and self-published a 36,000 word novella entitled The Trouble With Cash. The story took place in Costa Rica and I had fun using my first hand knowledge and experience.

I continued studying and learning more about creative writing and finished my first novel, Spirits' Gold, in 2018. While fictitious, it is inspired by some of my own extraordinary experiences while working in gold mines in the Ivory Coast and other out of the way places.

When I'm not checking on operations in the coffee farm with our three rescue dogs or entertaining guests in the lodge, I'm working on the storyline for my next novel.

Books by the Author

Spirits' Gold
The Trouble With Cash

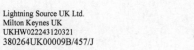